To My Boo
enjoy you
Lo

THE SAVIOR

DEEP IN MY THOUGHTS

P N PICARD

Published in United Kingdom by:

Qoatz
Email: p.np@qoatz.co.uk
Website: www.qoatz.co.uk

Cover Design by **Kysha Marie Buffong**
www.keewimedia.com

Layout and Interior Design by
Manish Pathak

Edited by **Elizabeth Whrite**

First printed in August 2019

Distributed and printed by Ingram Spark
www.ingramspark.com

ISBN 978-1-9161935-0-5

CONTENTS

PROLOGUE

I'M RACING…I'M RACING against time. I have to make it. I must get to her…

I would never forgive myself if I failed. I refuse to fail.

For as long as I can remember, we have always been together, joined as one… I still don't remember my life before her; but I feel like it was always leading to her, to be by her side somehow. We are connected – I can sense that now.

All those nightmares were because of her. I was sensing her, feeling her pain. How I didn't see it sooner haunts me. All this time wasted. What if they kill her? What if he goes against his word just to be fucked up? What if…?

I remember the look on his face when I appeared right there, right in front of him. I still have no idea how I was able to do it or how I was able to control it. I just remember focusing on her.

Remembering the faith she had in me. The next thing I knew, poof, and I was there. Then I was right in front of him, delivering instructions.

He wasn't the one in charge. He wasn't Michael, but he was guarding the place where she was. That was all I cared about.

All this practice and preparation had better have been worth it…because, one way or another, I will save her and kill whatever gets in my way!

CHAPTER ONE

'WHAT IS REAL?'

IT'S DARK. I can't see, I can't see a thing. Thump, thump, thump! The sound of my heart is beating so fast through my chest. I'm scared, struggling to hear, struggling to concentrate on the sounds of my surroundings.

'Ssshhh!' I mumbled to myself. Inhale, exhale, inhale, exhale, I kept repeating. There we go, calm and still – as if I were air; no, as if I were non-existent. I hear something – voices? What are they saying? Where are we going? Are they taking me to where she is?

Now, we have stopped. I know we have – I can feel it. Come on, Alexa, it's now or never. You need to get away. The car is moving again, but slowly. I can feel everything; I can hear everything – the sound of oil bubbling in the engine. The needle on the speedometer, we are moving at 30 miles an hour. How am I doing this? What is happening to me? What's wrong with me? Am I seriously asking myself questions in sequences of three?

'Now, Alexa!' my mind screamed at me. My heart began to race with such speed. Thump, rolling, rolling, then stop. The pain I felt in my body was beyond words. There was no time for that – I pulled off the bag that was over my head. I could see from a distance that the car was turning around, coming back for me. Ignoring the pain, I began to run for my life…

"Alexa, Alexa – WAKE UP, WAKE UP!"

I heard the sounds fading in and out of my ear... hmmm, am I dreaming? My eyes opened, vision distorted, blurred. I was in a somewhat dark room, "where am I?" I thought, my head aching with pain. I sat up slowly, my hand pressed against my head, empty bottles of vodka and brandy, an ashtray full of weed and cigarette buds were all I could see at first.

"Oh, I am at home," I thought. Then my memories came to me... we were out last night partying away like we always do on Friday nights. We must have come back here... Yes, we brought the party home; we were so wasted. I got up slowly, smiling to myself as I remembered bits of last night's events. I hear something, what is that noise? Is that crying?

As I heard the cry, I looked around, and to my shock, I saw Jenna standing in the corner with a butter knife in her hand, pointing towards me. "What the hell are you doing?" I asked. "Aargh, my fucking head is killing me." As those words left my lips, Jenna dropped the knife and ran towards me, right into my arms and held me tight. I suddenly pulled away from her, confused, but before I could say anything, my head pain got worse. Yes, my head was killing me and not due to the effects of alcohol, not because I was wasted; this was no hangover. This was different, something I had been suffering from for years, well as long as I could remember. I would get these attacks...

I remember one night I was sleeping, I woke up in a cold sweat, my head started aching, and this was no ordinary headache – the pain felt like I had been hit with a chrome bar repeatedly. I also began to see things, and then my nose would bleed. Sometimes, the images would be fuzzy like watching a pirate DVD where the cameraman is moving all the time, and the lens of the camera is filthy. And some dreams would be visible, seem so real as if I was projected right there at that moment.

I visited so many different doctors, I spoke to therapists, was prescribed to so many different pills to stop the pain but nothing worked. I even had a brain scan once. They said the structure of the left side of my brain was abnormal or some shit like that. I walked out after a while when they were in the middle of discussing my results; it was out of anger as it was clear the doctors didn't have a clue what was wrong with me.

Jenna dragged me to a psychic once, the lady touched my hand and freaked out, screaming out all these weird words, saying I was chosen. I thought it was nothing but hokum and realized that if the doctors, the therapist or the 'psychic' couldn't help me, no one could. I decided to sketch down what I saw in my dreams, or should I say my attacks, to see what they meant. I wasn't that bad at drawing, so that helped, but after a while of looking through some of them, I could never understand what they meant, so I lost interest. This led me to my next option, cannabis, I did some research and apparently, cannabis... well, the THC, cures cancer by aiding with killing the cells and also helps with pain... well, that's what was said on a website, so I thought, "what the hell, I've tried everything, this may help to ease the pain."

Well, that's what I hoped for. It helped for a while... Well, I thought it did as the attacks had stopped, but who knows, I might have been too high to notice they were there. But after some time, they came back. I felt them, but I still kept smoking. I liked getting high. What can I say? So yes, that's my story.

Jenna was shaking so much that I was beginning to move with her. 'What the hell? What happened? What's wrong?' I asked. I always asked in a sequence of three, whatever the subject. She just kept looking at me; the fear in her big blue eyes had me worried.

Jenna and I went way back. We grew up together; she was my best friend, my sister, and my rock. We met and grew up in a children's home, called the Roman Catholic Orphan Asylum, a very strict home run by a group of prestige nuns. I know you're thinking, 'how did someone like me come from a Catholic home...' well, I did. I read the Bible every day – we were taught the history of the Bible, not much on universal history life – we followed the rules of the text, and if anyone disobeyed, they were sent to solitude. Strangely, it was an orphanage where no one ever visited to adopt; we were just to be raised and leave on the 21st birthday; weird, I know. I later learned that it was a sham of some sort and they had breached so many acts that I knew to be possible. Even after extensive research, the actual leading franchise had shut down or evolved into something else years ago. I was so shocked when I came to learn these things; then again, it did explain why it was so secluded.

Something I always thought about during my time there. I remember the strictest of all nuns, Sister Beridith Clarke. Oh, she was a mean, frightening woman. Oh, how much I hated her, and hate is a strong word, but I've always used it so freely with her. She made my life a living hell, the number of times she shunned me to solitude just because she didn't like my opinion about things. The number of times she beat me with her unique cane when she felt isolation wasn't enough punishment. I'm glad to be free of her and that place, good riddance! But yes, back to Jenna and me. We also left together, or we like to say, escaped from the system at the age of 17. Five years later, and we are still going strong, have always had each other's back. Or more I had hers, as she is so small, 4ft 5 to be precise.

She was always small. I remember the first day we met; she was the tiniest in the home we shared. A small frightened girl with brown curly hair, little freckles on her cheeks, which she claims to be beauty spots, not freckles, as she hated that word, and big blue eyes. I can always read her by looking into her eyes; that's what drew me to her, and I have never left her side since. Nothing's changed about her now, except for her height, and even though she is still small and she has gone through puberty, she still has the same curly brown hair just a bit longer and fuller and the blue eyes that I can always read.

I remember, once a day, the nuns would go off to have their prayer meetings, while we had, I don't know, let's call it recess. They would always leave one nun in charge, Sister Gracey Anny Mey, who was the oldest of the sisters. Her coordination and focus weren't what it used to be, and she would often fall asleep on the horrible white rocking chair she practically lived in. Each day, thirty minutes into recess, Sister Mey would fall asleep then Jenna and I would go off to our secret spot and talk about the world and things for the remaining forty-five minutes. We would make up stories about who our parents were and why they left us. I used to joke that Jenna's were a family of dwarfs and they disowned her because she was too tall. She hated that joke, and she would get me back by saying I was left because I was mix-raced and my mother was either white and scared that her family would disown her for sleeping with a black man, or black and ashamed for sleeping with a white man that left her hanging.

Yes, what a bitch so small but had such a sharp tongue on her. I would laugh it off and say it's the twentieth century and it's less likely that would be the scenario, but deep down, it would bother me and my mind would wander. Why did my mother never want me? Why don't I remember her? I came to the orphanage at the age of six, but till this day, I have no memory of what my life was like before.

I never told Jenna about it. I just said I never knew her when we first had that conversation, and I never let her know it bothered me. I didn't want to make her feel bad, she had a sharp tongue and said things that got us into a lot of trouble many times, but she was still my best friend, my sister, my rock. She would always be by my side even when the attacks started... she knew everything.

As I looked into those big blue eyes, I could see the fear taking over her. I could see something had frightened her to death; she had seen something so horrific and sick. The expression in her face, her body language was not how it should be. I have been around this girl for 16 years, I have watched her grow up into the person she is now, and I knew something was really wrong. Her eyes focused on mine then her mouth opened then closed once again. Confused, I looked away and started to look around and realized how dark it really was in this room – the curtains were closed, and the two doors were shut. The only source of light was a small lamp that was abandoned in one of the corners of the room.

Jenna and I didn't live a luxury life, we came from nothing, so we made the best of what we had, and what we had was a small studio apartment. One room that we shared, one sofa futon bed, a box TV in the corner that rested on a second-hand wooden table that we actually found in the alleyway a few blocks from our home. It was a bit chipped when we found it, so I filed it down and painted it with some varnish. We had a table and chair that we found too, and we shared a wardrobe. We paid for the wardrobe and bed; of course, we are not tramps.

Jenna worked at Marlitos Marlos' bar. Yes, the name is a little odd, it was a small bar hidden in the nightlife of New York City, as we lived in the city. I actually pitied the owner when I learned that it was his real name. I felt that his parents were pricks for giving him such a name that any kid would find a way to make fun of. I am sure he had a terrible childhood because of it, but surprisingly, he turned out to be a good man. Well, he had to be, after giving Jenna a job when he knew she had no experience. But weeks after starting, she became a natural behind the bar. There was something about being able to mix drinks and seeing their effect on people that excited her; her eyes would always light up when a punter got wasted from one of her cocktails. I think in her own little creepy way, she felt like she was this mad scientist or something, I don't know. She is a weirdo like that.

And myself, well, I hustled whenever I could, and most of the time, I found myself at Marlos so I could keep an eye on Jenna, just in case something happens. I have always felt like I needed to protect her. There had been a few occasions where I would step in when a punter got too crazy from one of Jenna's cocktails and felt like being a little touchy, feely. You might as well say I was the security guard that was not on a legitimate payroll. Marlos never complained about it; it didn't bother him as he loved Jenna for bringing in the punters and it intrigued him to see a woman such as myself being able to throw a man out the bar.

I wouldn't say I am strong, but being 6 foot was an advantage, especially when the punters were intoxicated. I also hustled sometimes when playing the bar games like darts and pool. I would always win and flirt a little too, so it's a win-win. It's not the most exciting life, but it's ours, and we can do as we please without having to worry about Sister Clarke and her minions breathing on our backs.

I continued to look around while still stuck in time, thinking about Marlitos Marlos.

'Where is my phone,' I suddenly thought to break out my trance down memory lane. I looked back at Jenna; she was still and quiet. I looked into her eyes.

'What time is it? Why is it so dark? What happened?' I asked in my sequence of three.

"It's 6 o'clock," she said.

'What?! in the morning,' I said angrily. 'why in the hell did you wake me.'

"No, no, in the evening," she stuttered, interrupting me, then before I could comment back, she started repeating these words over and over. "It wasn't a dream; the end is here. It wasn't a dream; the end is here."

'What the fuck' I gasped as I stepped back all freaked out, which was an overreaction, I know, but in the 16 years I had known this girl, she had never acted like this before. And I watched a lot of scary films that's traumatized me for a lifetime; I thought this shit was getting way too creepy. Jenna kept repeating it again and again. 'Jenna, Jenna,' I shouted as I reached out and grabbed her shoulders, but she carried on chanting.

Really, I thought and did what any reasonable person would do -- 'smack'

I slapped Jenna across her face.

"Ouch you bitch, what the hell?" She winced.

'I am sorry, but you were starting to scare the shit out of me,' I said as I loosened my grip on her shoulders and stood back a bit after letting go of her.

"I am sorry," she said as she walked over to the futon and sat down.

'You didn't answer my other two questions,' I said in an angry tone.

For some time, I had this thing where I asked in a sequence of three questions, and they had to be answered in the order they were asked; it had to be one after the other, no matter what was asked or how long the answer was, it had to be done. It irritated the hell out of Jenna but not more than it annoyed me. If it couldn't be done, something would come over me; I would get agitated, sweaty palms then become erratic. I thought it to be some form of OCD (Obsessive compulsive disorder), but Jenna told me it was YHDI, she never went into as what it was, and if there was a cure, so for weeks, I did research and more research.

I went to libraries, hospitals, doctors but no one had answers, then one day she put me out of my misery and told me YHDI stood for You Have Deep Issues and laughed in my face. That day, I could have taken her life and not cared. I was so angry, I was furious I had wasted weeks researching something that I thought was a scientific name, but no, it was Jenna being a bitch because it annoyed her the way I ask questions.

After several months of calming down, I was able to forgive her, and in all truth, I was able to agree with her. I did have YHDI for the simple fact that I didn't always ask questions in a sequence; it just started one day, and I haven't stopped since. I do not know what happened that day or really remember too tough on what could have triggered it, which is a mystery to me, just like many things in my life I do not understand. "O," she said, interrupting my thoughts. "I, I, and I," she began to stutter.

'Jenna, what the hell man, you're freaking me the fuck out,' I shouted. 'I wake up to you holding a knife to me, well a butter knife, the house is dark, and then you start chanting shit.'

"Ssshhh," she whispered as she jumped up from the bed and shoved me against the wall.

'What did you see,' I whispered back. Jenna knew I was going to ask another two questions, so before I could open my mouth, she began to stutter.

"I, I, I woke up early this morning and I felt cold freezing, remember we came with Ric, Jae and Tracey last night?

Ric, Jae, and Tracey our good friends... ok, more Jenna's than mine. Ric and Jae work at Marlos with Jenna, and Tracey is Ric's partner. They were the only three people that we knew and grew close to... Our little circle of trust Jenna often referred to us when we all would be together getting wasted. I found it bit gay, to be honest, but hey, she loved it, and it didn't irritate me enough to complain about it. Ric found it corny too, while Tracey loved it as much as Jenna did so they would sometimes do a little dance to go with it. Jae would always join, even though deep down I knew he couldn't stand it but did it for Jenna's sake. I had always known he had a thing for her, but Jenna's just oblivious to the thought. Ric is short for Ricardo Mendes and Jae for James Mendes, known as the Mendes twins. After meeting him the first time, Ric explained he was the older brother, well by five minutes to be exact. Apparently, Ric claims when in the womb just before his journey to planet earth, Jae's leg was dragged away, allowing him to come out first. It's the dumbest story I have ever been told I have no idea why I am even retelling it. But yes that is his story and he feels due to being the older twin he is more superior to Jae for having the upper hand, so when they are debating and even when Ric is wrong, the "older" twin is always right... It's quite sad, really but hilarious to watch. Hmm, Tracey... 'Wait' I thought... oh yeah, where are they? When did they leave? They did come back last night, didn't they?' I asked, scratching my head.

"I woke up, they were gone, and the front door was open," she said, and as she began to tell her tale, I saw the fear return in her eyes.

"I thought that was weird, why would they just walk out and leave the door open, but I was too hungry to go back to sleep and there was hardly anything in the fridge except for that stale cheese and a drop of milk, so I decided to go to the store. As I started to walk down the streets, I didn't realize at first because I felt so hungover," she said then hesitated.

'Go on,' I pushed.

"After a while, I started to look around and"...

She started to shake.

'Jenna, man,' I growled.

"Sorry, sorry, there were cars that were smashed, some had doors wide open with keys still in the ignitions, and I thought why people would leave the cars like that, something's not right."

'So you've freaked out about some cars, Jenna. Really?' I asked with the straightest stare I could do.

'Thump'

'ow,' I winced from her fist hitting my arm.

"You don't understand. As I walked further and furthermore, cars on the road were abandoned, on fire, there were even police cars too," she said, trying to control her emotions. "I don't know why, I don't know what possessed me, after all when I watch movies I complain about people exploring, but I continued to see what was going on and after passing a few more cars, I began to hear these moans, cries. I thought someone might be hurt, so I followed the sound." She could no longer hold it in, stuttering turned to her body shaking, shaking to trembling, then she broke down, eyes flooded with tears.

'Jenna, what did you see?' I pressed again.

"Ja, Ja, James, he was I, I, I don't know, I don't know he was, it looked like he was eating Tracey."

'Bah ha ha ha ha ha ha ha,' I burst out into laughter. That is the stupidest thing you have ever told me, nice try Jenna you actually nearly had me with the shaking and the stuttering. And that you've just seen a ghost look you got going on right now ha ha ha ha ha ha' I laughed again, but laughter soon turned to silence and my smile was gone, I was serious once I saw no change on Jenna's face. 'So you expect me to believe that there is apocalyptic zombie shit going on right now?' I asked, and before I could start my sequence, she cut me off once again.

"No," she said back, angry. "This was different, Jae's face and hands; they had changed."

'Yea, right' I rolled my eye, sat down on the bed, reached for my box, and started to roll my spliff. 'Smack'

Jenna smacked the weed out my hand.

'Jenna, you are testing my patience,' I shouted back at her.

"No, you don't get it, you lanky fool," she screamed back.

Yes, lanky fool, how I hated those words. Jenna would always call me that in an argument when she was outraged and wanted to make it known that she was not playing, I hated it so much I was quite sensitive at times towards my height, and she knew that.

"He had changed, his face looked deformed, and he looked exactly like one of your drawings," she said while disappearing into the passage and reappearing with boxes. Dropping to the floor on her knees, she went through the boxes, going through all my books, searching. "Here it is," she said then threw it in my face, which landed in my lap. Before I could respond, she came charging towards me, took the book off my lap and started flipping through to go back to the page she just found.

"Where has it gone? Where is it, ahhh," she mumbled to herself. Look, look." Waving it in my face, I took the book; it was a detailed sketch of a man, but it wasn't a man at all, his face was disfigured. It looked scary, like some sort of demon but still familiar, the eyes were dark, evil, but again those eyes, I knew those eyes. I had seen them before; they were Jae's. But how could this be? I drew this picture many years ago in my young life before I even met Jae, saw what he looked like, but this was him. I could see it so clearly now.

"This is what I saw... This was Jae," she said to me with her big eyes piercing at me. As I looked into her eyes, I knew then she wasn't joking with me, she meant what she said, but I refused to believe there were such things as demons to be true. This wasn't a movie; I was ignorant to the fact.

'This doesn't mean anything,' I said as I continued to make my spliff.

'You was wasted this morning; it was probably a figure of your imagination.'

"Alexandra Nemesia, I am not lying, I did not imagine these things. I am not crazy; this thing chased me. I have never run so fast in my life. It ran up a wall for fuck sakes," she grimaced at me. Whoa, she said my full name. She never says my full name. Only when shits going down like when we planned to escape the home Jenna said my full name. When we were squatting in some vacant flat when things were terrible, and we nearly got caught, she called out my full name. She hasn't called my name since then, but I looked at her, ignoring my thoughts, still being in denial and ignorant to what she was telling me.

'Prove it,' I said to her as I inhaled a pull from my spliff and blew it out and upwards to the ceiling. Jenna was mad; she paced back and forth, then got the TV remote and switched it on. I watched her with a confused expression, then to my shock looked at the TV.

Static after static, blue then black green, sound, silence, an irritating recurring alarm was what all I could see as I watched Jenna flick through the channels. Terror and anxiety took over me. I began to feel the room spinning; I felt light. I am either scared out of my mind, or this is some good shit that I am smoking, I put the spliff in the ashtray and Jenna noticed how uneasy I became and helped me sit back down on to the bed. 'What does this mean? I am freaking out, Jenna, I am freaking out,' I gasped as I started hyperventilating. In the movies when the TV is like that, it usually means that everything is fucked up and everyone is dead. Oh my gosh, everyone is dead, Jenna. Oh my god, I'm dying... we're going to die.' I started to cry.

"Ssshhh, calm down," she said as she looked into my eyes while resting both of her hands on my shoulders, grabbing me firmly. She then ran to the kitchen and came back quickly to me. "You are not dying; you are high. Drink some water. You need to sober up. You're freaking out, calm down. I need you to relax, breathe in, breathe out and again; there we go; just keep doing that for me."

Jenna was right; I was high as a kite freaking out. Her breathing technique was actually working, or I was still high and just passed the paranoid stage, who knows, but I started to calm down.

"You ok? I need you to be, Alexa, I can't do this without you," she said as I continued to breathe in and out.

'Yes, I am good. I don't know why I got like that,' I said to her, but I was lying. I knew precisely why I got like that. The picture I sketched many years ago was real; Jenna saw it; how could that be? What is happening?

"Alexa... Alexa," Jenna called. I snapped out of it and saw her staring right in my face.

'Yea, I was just thinking,' I replied.

"About what?" she asked.

'Erm that'... I hesitated.... 'that you didn't answer my third question, nor did you explain it in the correct order.' I wasn't ready to admit that I believed her. I needed more proof.

"Really, Alexa?! I just told you something, and you want to come at me with that repetitive shit?" she barked. I stared at her. "Fine, I apologize that I answered incorrectly," she said while grinding her teeth. "It is dark because I was afraid that there were others like Jae, so I barricaded the front door, closed the others and kept the curtains closed, so no one would hear or see us, to prevent anyone from coming here."

'OK,' I said quietly as I struggled to process what I just heard. Jenna watched me as I sat in silence for a few minutes. I then got up and walked to the door that leads to the passage; I opened it and saw the wardrobe and a suitcase against the door. 'How did I not notice the wardrobe was gone from the room,' I mumbled to myself. I looked back at Jenna, I opened my mouth to speak, and before I knew it, I heard a sudden noise. It got louder, it crept up slowly, a silent ninja ready to make his move. Before I knew it, my mouth began to water. I knew what time it was, so I quickly ran into the bathroom and was sick in the toilet. Fear, shock, denial, or just effects from a hangover took over me, and that was the only way I could release it. Just as I finished and was about to flush it away, Jenna grabbed my hand. 'What are you...?'

"Ssshhh," she whispered before I could finish my sentence. She then helped me up and guided me back into the room, she sat me down then left but returned shortly with a basin of water and a wet rag, and she sat it on the floor beside me then walked over to the door and closed it slowly.

"Look, I understand you are struggling to take this in right now, and it's hard to believe, but we have to be quiet, Alexa," Jenna said quietly while walking over to me. I nodded back at her as I got the rag and began cleaning my face. "What are you thinking?" She asked.

'I don't know,' I replied.

"Don't lie, Alexa, I know you," she snapped back.

'OK, I lied. Do you want to know the truth? I'm thinking I am scared as shit,' I said back as I gurgled water in my mouth.

"OK, ok, acceptance, that's good. You believe me. It will be OK; we will get through this," she said as she patted my shoulder.

'You don't get it; I am scared as shit because what you saw today is something I drew a very long time ago, and if that has become a reality, how do we know that the other things that I have drawn will not become real as well?'

She opened her mouth then paused, "But not one of them drawings were, I don't know... good, happy. I can't remember all of them," she whispered to herself. "What do we do?"

'If this is really happening, we need to go through all of them... Now.' I said as I jumped up off the bed.

CHAPTER TWO

ACCEPTANCE

A FEW HOURS HAD passed, the silence between us. I looked over at Jenna, three books on the floor, and the fourth in her hand. Confused, frustrated, nothing made sense; there were so many drawings I don't even remember doing so much, so many pictures with no meaning – one with squares that looked like car windows, a broken clock, a license plate, a blurred speedometer, and others with lines and sketching. I couldn't take it anymore, so I threw the book on the floor, got up, and walked over to the bed to get my spliff. I laid back, lit it, and inhaled the biggest pull and exhaled, staring at the ceiling.

"What are you doing?" Jenna asked in an irritated tone.

'I am done, Jenna. I've had enough,' I said back. 'Nothing makes sense. I am starting to remember why I stopped going through these drawings years ago; I'm confused. All I see is squares, a speedometer, even a license plate, what the hell is that supposed to mean?'

Jenna looked back at her book then grabbed the others she was previously looking at. A few minutes had passed, and a little smirk appeared on her face, the type that I just figured it out and I feel like a smart-ass smirk.

'Spit it out, Jenna, I know you figured it out,' I said to her as I continued to smoke.

"Ok, ok I get what these are," she said as her smile began to get bigger. "You have done a drawing in a series of drawings."

'What, why, explain,' I said back more confused than I was before.

Jenna began ripping out the pages of all the books she had, then did the same to the one I left on the floor. After a while, she started spreading them out.

'Ok I think I get it, it's like a puzzle,' I said, feeling satisfied that I had cracked the case.

"Yes, you slowpoke, why don't you stop smoking and come help me figure this out," she said.

'Nah you're alright, you're good at those kinds of things; you know I am not the one for puzzles, and you are doing so well already,' I looked at her and smiled.

Jenna rolled her eyes at me, then continued to put pieces together.

Nearly an hour had passed, and Jenna was still working. I lied on the bed and watched her for a while then got bored, so I went back to the TV to see if there had been any change, but there was nothing. I looked back at Jenna. I looked at the pictures, and something about it was familiar, Deja vu?

'Wait, stop,' I said as I continued to stare at the pictures.

"What? Why?" Jenna asked, confused.

'I remember; I know this.'

I got down on my knees, and my hands took over, they moved so quickly, putting each picture in the correct place. I don't know how I was doing it; it was like it wasn't me, but it was. As each picture was set down, the image became clearer and more apparent, it felt so familiar looking at it, and I no longer felt confused.

'I know this; I remember this,' I whispered to myself.

"So do I," whispered Jenna.

We both stood up as I put the last picture in place and stood back and looked at the whole image. It was a series of drawings of one drawing – a person sitting in a car with a bag over their head. The detail was precise, the vehicle, its shape, its windows, the license plate, the speedometer, the driver and passenger... well, the back of them.

"I remember this dream," Jenna whispered again.

I looked at her, confused.

"It was the night after your 'nineteenth' birthday. You were talking in your sleep; you started sweating then shaking, then you woke up crying because you were in so much pain; usually, it's your head, but this time, you said your whole body was aching. When I asked you what you saw, you couldn't remember everything, but you drew a broken clock, then several nights after that and then months, it was still the same feelings but a different drawing, and you always mumbled the same thing just before you awoke," Jenna said as she looked at me.

'What did?'

"Now Alexa," she whispered, interrupting my sequence.

There was nothing but silence for a while; it was as silent as one of those old cowboy films where the town is deserted, and there is nothing but a ball of hey blowing by.

'I remember not remembering, if that makes sense. I remember being confused and scared, but I am not that confused anymore.'

"Why?" Asked Jenna.

'Because I had the same dream before you woke me; it was so clear, so vivid, so real,' I answered. 'This drawing, this person under the bag is me. I am the person.'

"How can you be sure? you might be wrong."

'I remember everything from the dream now. I had been taken. I was in the car with the bag, and it was so dark I couldn't see. I remember the car had stopped then started and was moving slowly, so I hopped out and was rolling and rolling. I told myself, 'now, Alexa' when I was about to jump out. I think I woke up in pain because of the rolling out the car, but I felt it all them years ago, and I didn't feel it today. This doesn't make sense.'

Jenna looked at me in shock as I tried to make sense of what I was saying, then there was a sudden noise.

"What was that?" Jenna shrieked as she got close to me, her eyes darting back and forth to each window and door, waiting for someone to come in.

'It was my stomach. I am starving,' I said embarrassed.

"Really, Alexa, the world's ending and you're thinking about food," she said as she pushed herself away from me.

'Well, what do you want from me? It's 10 o'clock in the evening and I haven't eaten a thing; you didn't even bring anything back from the store.'

Jenna put her head into her hands. “Jesus Christ,” she mumbled to herself, “I live with a complete idiot; no, Alexa, I was too busy running for my life I wasn’t thinking about food.”

‘So how we supposed to survive without food,’ I said all grumpy.

“Forget about that, we will think of something later,” she said while rolling her eyes and going back to the picture.

“Growl.”

The sound of my stomach began to echo throughout our tiny apartment.

‘I wish I could, but I can’t ignore this, Jenna, there must be something in the kitchen,’ I moaned. I walked towards the kitchen door, my hand nearly touching the handle. Jenna zoomed right behind me.

“Alexa. we need to be careful,” she whispered.

‘Ssshhh, I will ok, I will keep the light off. I am so hungry I do not care if the world is ending, I need to eat something, just wait there,’ I snapped back.

I disappeared into the kitchen, opening cardboard, door after door slowly and quietly as I could, hoping to find something.

‘Yes,’ I whispered to myself.

I found a pack of crackers, a jar of jam, and a bottle of water. I grabbed a knife, a saucer, and two cups, and entered the room. Closing the door behind me using my toe as I was struggling with all the items I had in my hands, I dashed to the bed and dropped them.

‘Phew,’ I thought.

After a few seconds, I realized Jenna was nowhere to be seen; my heart began to race.

‘Jenna,’ I called out quietly.

A few seconds had passed, and I was just about to freak out, but then I saw a little movement from the bed. Jenna's hands popped out from under the mattress as her body followed.

'Really, I go to the kitchen for a few minutes, and you hide underneath the mattress.'

"Well, you were the one that decided to risk getting caught for a packet of crackers and jam. I was just smart," she snapped at me.

I held my breath and counted to ten in my head to calm my nerves. I couldn't believe this girl chose to hide in the result of fear of me getting caught and killed in the kitchen, what a coward. I couldn't believe it; actually, I could. She is so small, bless her.

I sat down on the bed, took out my crackers, and begun spreading it with jam.

'Do you want some? How many? Any ideas?' I asked her.

Jenna rolled her eyes, "Yea why not, give me three, please. Any ideas on what?"

'Honestly, I wasn't sure. At first, I didn't know what to ask you for the third question, and I felt my eye beginning to twitch, so I just asked you for the sake of it, but now when I think about it, I am talking about the drawing,' I replied.

"Oh, Erm," Jenna began biting her lip as she stared at the big picture on the floor.

'Wa...'

"I am scared," she blurted out, interrupting me before I barely spoke.

"You drew something, or should I say someone a long time ago, someone who you never knew or had ever seen before who had become my friend, and I see him today, and he looked... he was, it well, was exactly how you had drawn it," she continued.

"Hmmmm," Jenna sighed and looked away from the picture; she sat right next to me and reached over for the spliff, ignoring the four crackers I had spread for her.

'Wow,' I thought. You see, Jenna wasn't much of a smoker like me; she would participate every once in a while, but it wasn't her thing. Now, look at her laying back inhaling and exhaling. I couldn't believe what I was seeing.

"Is it possible to already be high after two puffs?" do not even answer that question," she stuttered as I attempted to open my mouth.

Dropping the spliff back into the ashtray, Jenna walked over to the picture and what was left of my books. She started to pick up the covers of the current destroyed books and noticed there was one book left.

"There's one more," she whispered as she dropped to her knees.

"No I can't, I can't look in here. I am sorry, Alexa, this was the one with Jae's face; I don't even want to remember what else was in there."

She looked over at me; her eyes flooded with water. To her surprise, I was busy stuffing my face with the eighth cracker.

"Really Alexa, have you not eaten enough already? and I am sure you have moved on to mines," she snapped.

'I was so hungry, and I didn't think you wanted yours,' I blurted while stilling chewing on a piece of cracker.

"What?" Jenna said in a confused tone.

'I said sorry,' I lied after swallowing the last piece of cracker and gulping down my last glass of water.

"You're not taking this seriously, and I am freaking out Alexa, maybe you're right, you know, maybe I did imagine it this morning with the whole Jae thing, it's not like we've heard any sirens, and the TV is probably broken. what was I thinking?" Jenna said before bursting out with laughter.

I walked over to her and put my hand on her shoulder and looked into her eyes.

'Jenna, you didn't imagine it; it was real, this is real, you are just high and freaking out. I told you that this was some strong shit, you need to sit down and eat some crackers, drink some water and sober the fuck up'.

"No, I am not high... well, maybe a little. I just refuse to believe this. How can I believe something I don't understand? I don't understand what this picture means, and you said it seems so clear to you when you were putting it together, right?" She asked.

'Yes,' I answered.

"What is clear? Please explain. Where was I? Where were you going? When? How?"

Question after question after question, wow it seemed like Jenna had the YHDI. At that moment, I knew how she felt; it was crazy.

"I want you to explain to me in detail from beginning to end about your dream."

'OK I will, but first, sit down and eat; your belly keeps talking,' I pushed.

Jenna walked over to the bed with me, sat down and started scoffing down the crackers like she hadn't eaten in days. For a moment, I began to wonder if she was lying and if I had been sleeping longer than said, then I realized that she just had the munchies and my worries disappeared.

'OK, I will start from what I can remember,' I began.

"Mmmmhmmm," Jenna hummed while stuffing her face.

'The dream starts with me in a car; I just remember knowing that I am in a car in the back seat, and it's dark. It is silent, but it isn't. I can hear my breathing, my heartbeat, so that is all I focus on. I inhale, and I exhale over and over like you taught me how to control my breathing, my heart begins to calm down, and there's nothing but silence. I begin to hear things that are impossible to hear; I hear oil and the water moving around in the engine, I can hear the needle moving on the car speedometer and pinpoint exactly where it is sitting, knowing what speed we are traveling,' I explain.

"Is that why you drew a blurred speedometer?" she asked as she stared at me like a child fascinated with what she was hearing.

'Yes,' I said. 'I could hear the drivers' heart... Well, I do not know what they were as the beating pattern was unusual, I felt nothing from them but coldness, and they never spoke, not even when the car stopped. I remember thinking if they are taking me to where she is, I assume that was what I was thinking about since you weren't with me. I don't know what happened to you. I remember the car stopped for just a moment and there was silence, then it began to move again. I knew that it was at 30mph. I don't know how but I just did, so interrupting my thoughts, my mind said, "now Alexa," and I was out of the car, rolling and rolling on the road.' I continued.

"But how did you get out of the car? Weren't your hands tied?" She asked

'They were, but I just felt something in me, and I don't know,' I stuttered. 'But after I stopped rolling, I got up and pulled the bag off my head, and my hands were already free. I remember the pain my body felt from what I assume to be the fall, but that didn't stop me as I saw that car turn around and I started to run for my life, and the pain was ignored.'

'That's it; it has always stopped there... well, that's where it stopped. This morning is the furthest I have ever gotten in that dream,' I said as I looked back at the picture.

Jenna was quiet; she seemed a bit sober but still quiet. I usually could read her, but this time, I was struggling, and I didn't like that feeling at all.

"It's not a dream, Alexa, this is obviously some premonition, vision, whatever you want to call it," she said as she got up from the bed. "You do know that, don't you? I know you just gave me details, but I still don't understand your drawings, your 'visions' – they are not straightforward enough."

'Really, how straightforward do you want them to be?'

"Bla, blah, blah, I haven't got time for question number two and three," she blurted out before I could continue. She had interrupted my sequence quite a few times now; it was starting to get to me. I could feel my eye beginning to twitch.

"Oh go smoke your crap to calm your nerves. I am not sorry, your pictures are stupid you've got a drawing here of you being kidnapped, how is that supposed to help us, we don't know why, when, or where."

Jenna went quiet, she rushed to the pile of book covers, picked them up, and started to look through them.

I opened my mouth then closed it again, thinking what's the point, she would just cut me off, and my eye was already twitching.

"In case you were itching to ask, I just remembered you drew a picture of a broken clock," she said as if she had heard my thoughts and was answering my question.

"Here it is," she mumbled. She set the picture down in the corner of the drawing.

"Do you see this?" she said as she stood up and backed away from the whole picture.

'Yes,' I whispered to her as I walked over.

"Is this saying, showing what I think it means?" she said in a high-pitched voice.

'Yes I think so,' I whispered back.

We both looked at each with fear in our eyes, our heads in sync as we turned to look at the broken clock against our wall.

"Alexa"

'Jenna.'

'Thump, thump, thump.'

CHAPTER THREE

THE VISITOR

'THUMP, THUMP, THUMP.'

"Who is that?" Jenna whispered

'I, I, I don't know,' I whispered back.

The loud thumps continued coming from the front door, echoing into our apartment.

"What are you doing?" Jenna whispered while tugging on to my arm, as I began to walk to the door that led to the passageway.

I looked back at her and put my finger to my mouth, signaling her to shut up. I picked up the first thing I saw, which was a boot, and opened the passage door quietly and slowly as I could.

'Thump, thump, thump,' the door went again, causing Jenna to jump and get even closer to me as she was already holding on to my wrist like a frightened child.

'Look whatever you are, demon thing, I have a gun, and I know how to use it, so just go away,' I shouted to the door.

I looked back at Jenna, her face was pale as an abandoned corpse, but her eyes were scorching at me for what I said. I knew what I said was dumb, but I had utterly panicked, so I shrugged my shoulders and turned back to the door.

"Alexandra Nemesia," a voice called out.

It sounded like a man; yes, it was a man's voice, but nothing about it seemed familiar. I did not know this man, but he knew my name.

"Alexandra?" He called out again.

"How do you know her name," Jenna shouted back, still hidden behind me.

'Jenna, what the hell,' I whispered as I turned around to look at her. She was not as pale as before, but still terrified. I opened my mouth again, but then I was interrupted by the voice.

"I have been searching for you for some time now, Alexandra, I know you don't know me, but you must let me in at once; time is of the essence."

'Who are you, what do you want, and how do you know my name?' I blurted out.

"I am a friend, and I have come to help you. I am sure you are aware of what has happened to mankind, I have no problem answering your questions, but we must go, they will be here soon," he answered, disregarding my last question.

My eye began to twitch repeatedly, 'you didn't answer my third question or answer my second properly,' I snapped.

I could feel Jenna rolling her eyes behind me.

"You could be one of those things, so give her one good reason why she should open the door," Jenna said, saving me from my sequence.

"OK, I will give you three; how long have you had the headaches," said the voice.

I didn't answer.

"They were never headaches; they were visions, and tell me, have you noticed anything different about yourself your senses, your strengths, your abilities?"

'Abilities?' "what is he talking about," I thought but remained silent.

"OK Alexandra, from the age of six, you have no recollection of anything before that time; it's blank to you, you have no memory of your life or mother, and you have never known why.... well, I can tell you if just let me in, please."

I was frozen, fear, shock, confusion had taken over me. How did this stranger know these things? especially when no one knew, not even Jenna knew about it.

I felt her eyes staring at me, and before she could say anything, I dropped my boot and began moving the suitcases out the way and dragged the wardrobe back into the room.

Jenna looked at me with so much fear in her eyes. I looked back at and nodded to show her it's okay. I walked over to the door, unlocked, and opened to see this stranger I had never seen before.

"Bless you," he said as he walked past both of us, letting himself into our room. Jenna and I looked at each other, probably thinking the same thing, 'the cheek.'

I thought about popping my head out, but Jenna shut the door so quickly, shutting down that idea and began walking but hesitated as if she forgot about the man and remembered he was there.

I walked in front of her and led the way into our room. My eyes met his gaze; his eyes were dark, filled with so many different emotions. I could read it – anger, fear, sadness, relief, hmmm, why?

His face, healthy... with stubble, you could see he had not shaved in a few days or had a good night sleep. Dark hair and as tall as I, his appearance, his attire was smart and you could tell he was from somewhere that had followed strict rules and regulations.

I could tell this by the way he carried himself, his posture, and the way he spoke when I heard his voice at the door. I looked at him from head to toe, his short dark hair that was slightly out of place but would have probably been neat on a typical day, his shirt and leather jacket. He was wearing formal black trousers with dark suede loafers that looked a bit worn out.

I began to think about what he said at the door, how he knew that, and at the moment, it hit me; was he my father? I noticed him watching me after I zoned out, I opened my mouth, ready to ask a question.

"I am not your father if that is what you are thinking, Alexandra," he said, shutting that thought down immediately.

"I meant what I said: I am here to help you; I promise you, I am not the threat."

'I believe you are here for a reason. I wouldn't have opened the door if I didn't,' I replied.

It didn't hit me right away that he was not even talking to me but Jenna till I followed where his eyes were looking and turned to my side to see Jenna holding the butter knife in her hand.

'Jenna, please relax, he is not one of those things, and he knows stuff about me, he may know why this is happening,' I said slowly, trying to meet her gaze as she continued to stare at him, holding the knife. Jenna slowly lowered her arm and gave it to me, not once did her eyes leave his.

'Right, so let's start with your name. What is your name, how did you find us, and why are you here?' I asked while turning away from Jenna.

The man stared at me with a confused expression, "do you always do that?" he asked.

I looked over at Jenna; my left eye started twitching, and my right hand started shaking. Jenna cut her eye at me, and I heard her take a deep sigh.

"Yes she always does it, you must answer her questions immediately in the order she asked it, one after the other, no matter how long each answer is. She will start freaking out. As you can see right now, her eye is twitching, and her right hand is shaking; sometimes, she even has panic attacks, and no, I am not kidding, this actually happens. I have witnessed it," Jenna replied. I could hear in her tone that she was embarrassed, irritated, and just straight pissed off for having to explain that.

"Hmm, interesting," he replied.

"OK, well let me respond before you freak out. my name is Corbin Cathy Michaels".

I took a big sigh. I could hear Jenna mumbling to herself. Knowing her, it was most defiantly something rude about me, but I didn't care, the twitching had stopped, and that was all that mattered. Then after a few seconds, I realized the name he said. I could feel the corners of my mouth begin to move; I exchanged a quick look at Jenna, and she was already waiting for me to look at her. I knew what she was thinking; the same thing that I was – Corbin Cathy Michaels was a horrible name; it was worse than Marlitos Marlo.

"It told me where to seek you. I am here to help you and keep you safe, so we must leave at once," he continued interrupting the comedy show I was creating in my head.

"It... Well, what the hell is it?" Jenna asked, all freaked out.

"Look, I will tell you everything and anything, but I must get you somewhere safe right away," he said in a stern tone.

I looked at Jenna; she looked back at me and nodded, 'why should we trust you?' Jenna asked, speaking for both of us.

"Because you have questions and I have the answers. Do you really want to die here, never knowing what they meant? What all of this meant?" he replied sharply.

I was quiet; I looked at Jenna then I looked at him, my eyes darted back and forth around the room. I began thinking about my past. I tried to remember when I was six years old before I came to the home and met Jenna, but there was nothing. He was right; I had to know.

'OK, we will come. I just need to get some things together. Jenna, go grab some of your things'.

I grabbed a bag and started stuffing it with things I thought I might need. I grabbed first the most important thing to me, my weed box. I threw a jumper and jeans and change of underwear, the rest of the crackers, the water, and picked up the last remaining book.

I threw on my boots and my biker jacket. 'Where's my phone?' I thought to myself. I began looking under the pillows, and I could feel Corbin watching me as I moved.

"I don't mean to pree, ladies, but we must hurry. If I could find you, then it won't be hard for those things to find us. What are you looking for, Alexandra?" said Corbin.

"I am ready, actually," snapped Jenna.

'I am looking for my phone, and please call me Alexa,' I said.

"Your phone... why on earth would you need your phone?" Corbin said in an irritated tone.

'Where is it, where is it, ah there it is, I need it for exactly this,' I said as I started taking a picture of my drawing. We need to keep this, it's essential.'

"Why, what is it?" Corbin asked.

'Me being taken,' I replied as I shoved my phone in my pocket.

"I would ask how but there is no time for that, we must leave now," he said then walked out the room to the front door.

After unlocking the door, Corbin opened it slowly and popped his head out; he then signaled us to follow him. He led us to small black vehicle golf to be precise, the rush to the car seemed pointless as it was so quiet on the streets, deserted, not a person in sight.

The moment we got in the car, I was beginning to regret it. I didn't want to drive off with this stranger, a big part of me was hoping that this was just a bad dream and I was going to wake up any moment now, but no, this was real. Corbin had already said on the way to the car that it was going to be quite a drive to his 'secret' location, so I smoked the remainder of my spliff, threw the bud out the window and laid my head on Jenna's lap and allowed my mind to wander as we took off.

'Ssshhh,' inhale, exhale, inhale, exhale, there we go. I am calm and still; I am air, no, I am non-existent. I hear something, voices? What are they saying? Where are we going? Are they taking me to where she is? We have stopped, I know we have, I can feel it. Come on, Alexa, it's now or never... you need to get away. The car is moving again slowly, and I can see everything, I can hear everything; the sound of the oil bubbling in the engine, I can hear the needle from the speedometer, we are on 30mph, how am I doing this? What is happening to me?

'Now, Alexa'!!

The car came to a Holt, my eyes opened. I could feel Jenna tapping me gently. I was dreaming; it was the dream, the same one but different somehow.

'I am awake,' I said, my throat was dry, and I was confused.

I sat up and looked around me. It was still dark, was I not sleeping for long? Did I sleep for the whole day?

'Where are we? What time is it? Are you ok?' I asked in my three.

"Man, that is annoying," Corbin said as he turned around to look at me.

I jumped a little, 'I forgot you were here, I forgot where I was,' I said, staring at him while rubbing my eyes in between.

"We have gone through a tunnel that is I have no idea, ask Corbin, it's 4 o'clock in the morning, and I am alright. I know you were running out of questions, but thanks for asking anyway," Jenna replied while patting me on my shoulder.

Corbin stepped out of the car and began walking. Jenna and I hesitated then looked at each other, frozen in silence.

"Why are you still in the car? Let's move," he shouted.

'This man is really testing my patience,' I muttered.

"His people skills are disgusting," Jenna muttered back as we stepped out the car and followed.

What felt like hours but was only a few minutes that had passed, we came upon a steel door. Corbin zipped down his leather jacket and pulled out a silver chain, with a key at the end, and to my shock when I saw the white collar around his neck.

'Shit, you're a priest,' I blurted out.

"Alexa," Jenna snapped.

"It's complicated," he muttered under his breath while opening the big steel door.

As he walked in, I hesitated and pulled Jenna back as she was about to follow.

"What the hell," she moaned.

'Jenna, this guy is a priest. I smoked weed in front of a priest,' I said, trying to keep calm.

"I know; I know, I was holding a knife to him."

'A butter knife.'

"You're never going to let that go, are you?"

'We had other knives there, and you picked up a butter knife with jam on it.'

"Erm, ladies can we take this inside?" Corbin interrupted.

It was like embarrassment was a person, and they had just slapped me across the face. I couldn't even look at him nor Jenna, I walked passed him so quickly, keeping my head down.

I could hear him locking the door right after Jenna followed behind me. I decided to take my eyes off the ground and was amazed at what I saw when I did, his house, place, lair, whatever it was cool, I know that I am corny for saying it, but it was.

It looked like a cool secret hideout superheroes have in the movies where they keep their costumes and their gadgets, there were bookcases everywhere, a fireplace, tall windows but they were blocked with silver doors, sofas that looked comfy, a medieval-looking dining table and chairs, spiral stairs that lead to god knows where, and loads of portraits and paintings.

'So do you have a, err... is there somewhere I can freshen up?' I asked as I held my head back, staring at the ceiling.

The ceiling was exciting but quite disturbing; it was covered in paintings, some were beautiful, the detail, the colors, it was so defined. Others... Well, they were not that nice to look at; they were creepy; it was like reading a story through pictures. The one that caught my eye that compelled the most beauty was the birth of an angel; she was beyond words. Painting after painting showed her growth, more surprising after the next. As I continued to look at the others, I found myself feeling uncomfortable; the pictures were changing; they were dark, the angel seemed alone and afraid. Everything...everyone around her, that she cared for, she was losing them. I could see the pain in her eyes; those eyes seemed so real I looked away. I couldn't take it anymore, the story started to feel familiar somehow, plus my head and neck were aching from being held back for so long.

"Alexandra..."

'Huh,' I thought, I looked over to Jenna, but her mouth was closed.

"Alexandra," it was Corbin.

'Yes,' I replied.

"I was talking to you, you weren't quite here, were you?" he asked.

'Err, I, no I wasn't, but yes, I asked you something.'

"Yes, I was saying through the white door, take a left then a right, you will see a black door which will lead you to the lavatory," he replied.

I looked at Corbin, no expression, no sound, just silence. My gaze met Jenna's, still silent.

"Jesus, lavatory is bathroom, Alexa," she answered as if she had just read my mind.

'Oh, of course, I knew that. I was'...

I didn't even bother to finish my sentence; there was no point; we all knew I didn't know. I held my head down in shame and walked towards the white door and left the room.

"Did you notice she did not question me in her sequence of three?" Corbin pointed out to Jenna.

'You're right, she didn't, how strange' she agreed.

"How is that possible?"

'I have no idea, she has been doing it for so many years, and you have already witnessed how she reacts when it's not done correctly, but she didn't even ask all three questions,' Jenna added.

"Yes, right, but did it come to your attention that this happened while Miss Alexandra was looking at the ceiling?".

'Yes, yes, but why? It is only paintings; how could that distract her?' she asked Corbin.

"I understand we are nothing but strangers to each other in this poor forsaken tragedy, but you can trust me, and I will explain. Let us wait for Miss Alexandra first," he replied sternly as he walked over to the fireplace and turned it on.

'It's Alexa.'

"Excuse me."

'Call her by Alexa, she prefers that,' said Jenna.

"Very well then, Miss Jenna, and may I make a small request... can you please not speaketh thy Lord's name in vain?" he said as he watched the flames in the fireplace.

Jenna's face went bright red, so ashamed, so embarrassed she quickly nodded her head, no care or aware if he was looking and headed swiftly towards the white door.

Ten minutes had passed, and I am still struggling to work this damn shower, it was not like your standard modern type, it was very traditional. I already wasted five minutes trying to figure out how to flush the toilet, which was not even a toilet but something where water flies out of. I have never seen such a complicated thing in my life.

I was beginning to get annoyed and impatient, 'why won't you just work?' I screamed in the shower. Suddenly, the shower turned on, and the right temperature came out.

'Hmmm that was weird,' I muttered to myself, but I didn't care. I smelled foul like shit, vomit, and alcohol, so I hopped right in, no questions asked.

Specks of water hit my face and my hair, then traveled down my body. I stood there, lost in my thoughts, thinking about the paintings, the story, why did it get to me so much? Why did it feel so familiar? What did this all mean? I was so tired and frustrated, tired of being frustrated, so frustrated from not knowing and wanting to know.

'Knock, knock.'

The sound of the tapping on the door brought me back from the place I allowed my mind to wander to.

'Yes?' I called out.

"Alexa," it was Jenna. "Alexa, are you okay? You have been gone for some time now."

'Yea, I'm fine,' I lied. 'I was having trouble with the plumbing."

"Oh, Lex, you moppet," she giggled.

'I'll be out in a minute, just wait there. I need to show you something'.

After a few minutes of washing, I turned off the shower, dried off, and threw on the clean clothes I had packed before we left. I walked over to the mirror; I looked at my face, my eyes, my lips, and my nose. I felt odd; I looked weird. Staring into my own eyes, I began to feel the way I felt when I was staring at the paintings on the ceiling. I felt happy, full of joy. I was feeling this way as I gazed upon the birth of the new angel, such beauty. I felt beautiful, just like the...

'Knock, knock.'

I walked over to the door and let Jenna in.

"What did you want to show me?" she asked as she looked around the bathroom.

'I tried to release earlier.'

"Errrr," Jenna cut me off.

'No, no, not that,' I interrupted, defending myself. 'I went number one actually but yes I tried to flush the toilet, and the water went flying everywhere, it nearly went in my mouth, eww.'

Jenna burst out laughing; she laughed so much her eyes started filling with tears.

'What is so funny,' I asked angrily.

"It's not a toilet, it's a bidet," she replied while still laughing.

'A what?'

Jenna's laugh got bigger and louder, "a bidet, Alexa, it is like a toilet, but it is to wash your... You know."

'You know what? Oh, I see, eww, don't roll your eyes. How was I supposed to know that? How do you even know that?'

"Well, unlike you, I read and watch TV with posh shows," she said, grinning back at me.

'Bla, blah, blah, go shower you stink, I'll meet you upstairs,' I said as I closed the door behind me.

I re-entered the big room, or as I like to call it, the 'secret corner,' and Corbin was nowhere to be seen.

'Corb,' I called out.

"I am over here, Miss Alexa," I heard him call out, but I still couldn't see him. "Up here, I mean."

I looked up, and Corbin was on another floor going through books. I totally forgot about the spiral stairs in the left corner of the room.

"Do not worry yourself, I will be down at once, I just require some information," he said in response to my thoughts as if he heard the debate that was going on in my head. Was I really that easy to read, or was I thinking out loud?

"I see you have given me a nickname," he said, smiling as he walked down the spiral stairs. "I feel like I am a part of... What do you kids call it today? Posse, crew?"

'Wow, Oh God I just couldn't be asked to say your full name,' I replied, slightly feeling awkward. 'And do not ever use the word posse again.'

Corbin's expression quickly changed, and his speech was serious again, I know I hurt his feelings, but that was just weird; he is a priest for Christ's sake.

Clearing his throat, Corbin walked over to the fireplace and sat down; he then looked over at me.

"Are you ready to know the truth?" he asked.

'Yes, but we must wait for Jenna,' I replied.

"She can join us once she is available."

'No, I do everything with her; she needs to be here for the beginning.'

He nodded while looking at me; I think he knew I was adamant about waiting for Jenna. Shortly after, Jenna entered the room into an awkward silence.

"What is going on?" she asked.

'We were waiting for you so he can start telling us what is happening,' I replied.

'Corbin, we are ready now.'

"Very well then, here it goes..."

CHAPTER FOUR

'ASK AND THOU SHALL RECEIVE'

THE SILENCE BETWEEN all of us sitting around the fireplace. I looked over to Jenna; she looked to me. I looked at Corbin, and he was looking at me. I began to open my lips, ready to ask questions (crack), a sudden noise interrupting me. My heart began to race. I looked at Jenna to see if she was okay. Very irritated to what I saw next, Jenna stuffing her face with the crackers I had brought along with us, I looked at her my eyes filled with rage. Starring back at me, a piece of cracker hanging from her lips, "sorry," she whispered.

'Oh, my apologies, you must be starving' Corbin interjected. 'I'll get some food right away.'

'No!' I shouted. 'Sorry, no, thank you, food is not important right now, these questions that need to be answered are.'

"Okay, where would you like me to start?" He asked.

I could feel Jenna's eyes on me; she knew what my first question would be.

'Who is my mother? Why did she leave me? Where is she?' I asked in my sequence of three, anxious for the response.

"Alexandra, I am sorry to disappoint you," Corbin answered, "But you... I do not know how to say this".

"Then just say it," said Jenna.

"I cannot say where she is, but I can tell you why you were left," he continued.

I could hear Jenna muttering, and I knew why she was annoyed as much as I was, and she didn't even ask the questions. My eyes began to twitch; I started to grind my teeth.

'You haven't answered all my questions and not even in the right order,' I said as my eye twitched repeatedly.

"I know," he replied.

Jenna and I looked at each other in shock; she was as angry as I was. Before he could respond, Corbin got up and started pacing back and forth near the fireplace.

"I, I, Miss Alexandra, I cannot tell you her location, or tell you whom she is, as there is no her."

'I.... don't understand,' I interrupted. I could feel Jen's hand squeezing my shoulder.

"There is no her; you do not have a mother," he continued. "It is hard to explain; you are, I." Corbin stopped talking midway in his sentence, he put his hand to his chin, he went quiet; it seemed like he was thinking of the best way to make us understand.

"Okay, do you see the paintings on the ceiling?" He asked.

'You haven't answered my questions, and now you are asking me a question,' I snapped back at him.

"Please, Alexandra, just work with me here."

'Ok, yes I do,' I grunted.

"What did you feel when you were staring at it the whole time?" he asked.

"Why do you ask?" Jenna interrupted.

Corbin raised his hand to silence Jenna. "Alex."

"They are beautiful,' I said, cutting him off. 'I feel sad, pain, it feels familiar to me somehow, like I know this story.'

I could feel Jenna watching me; I looked at her, confusion written over her face.

"It feels familiar to you because it is you; this is not just a painting but a prophecy of your life."

"You see the baby, right?" he asked, I didn't even answer him; I just nodded as my eyes traveled to the ceiling to the first painting of the baby, my eyes fixed on hers.

"You see the baby has just been born, but was not barred from a woman or man or animal, just born, well, that is you."

'What are you saying?' Jenna whispered as her eyes were glued to the ceiling.

"That she has no parents," he replied. "She....

'What am I?' I interrupted.

'If I was born from no one, why am I mixed race? Am I real?' I continued.

"Many years ago, it was prophesied that a being would be born, protected by many till they reached 22 years of age. During adolescent life, the being would receive the gift of true sight, experiencing visions, to be precise; these visions were sent to prepare them for their day of battle. Alexandra, you are not mixed race nor black or white, but a representation of all cultures in the world, nor man nor woman but both, you have been given the ability to be able to feel others and to have so much strength no one has ever seen, you are our protector, and yes, you are real. I have waited for this moment my whole life, and it is an honor to be the one to share this knowledge with you."

'This is absolute bull crap,' I said while walking around the chair I was sitting on.

"Alexa," Jenna gasped. "Do not be rude; just hear him out."

'Are you listening to this? you expect me to believe that I am some protector,' I shouted back. 'That I have no mother, no father, I just appeared out of nowhere,' I said as I imagined myself popping out of a ball of smoke like an animated cartoon.

'What so God just clicked his fingers and I appeared in a manger.'

"Alexa," gasped Jenna.

'No sorry, not sorry, where is God in all of this? You say I was supposed to be protected, why was I abandoned at the age of six? Why don't I remember anything before that? Why did he make me?'

"It is okay, Jenna, I understand it is a lot for one to take in, and I would not blame you Miss Alexandra if you do not believe me, but I am not here to cause trickery," said Corbin. "I cannot speak for our Lord but speak for the believers that sent me on this mission; I was sent here to be a guide and protector, miss, just for a moment think about what I have shared with you, it does make some sense, does it not?"

'Firstly, my name's Alexa, and what makes sense? Because you knew about my dreams. I think not,' I said while rolling my eyes.

Corbin hesitated, cleared his throat then spoke,

"Sorry, I was not sure if that was a question or statement."

'What difference does it make?' I muttered to myself.

"If you noticed, which your friend and I already have, since you have been here and started making sense of things, you have not requested answers in a sequence of three as much."

Lost in thought, I sat down. I refused to look at him; I didn't realize that I had not asked the way I usually do. Did this mean that my repetition was due to my wanting to know about my past, and it was affecting me subconsciously?

"Alexan... Alexa," Corbin called out, quickly correcting himself. "You were protected when you were born and raised and trained by people who cared for you deeply, but the evil was getting strong, corrupting people close to us, and there was a great risk of you being found. So the safest thing to do was to send you away and put into care with your memories removed. It was a chance to have a normal life, actually, an idea formed by my father, he thought you deserved to experience the world as we did, to become in touch with humanity before you had to grow up and live this burden."

'So your father thought it was a great idea to send me to an orphanage home with no memory of who I was. And start a new life that led me to homelessness, hungry nights, no money, nothing, well what an idiot... when do I get to meet him?' I said as my eyes darted back and forth to the ceiling and walls.

Corbin cleared his throat as he tried to control himself from his emotions taking over.

"Erm, he is dead just like the others; they are all dead. I am the last of our people."

'OH,' I replied. I felt terrible, a silly fool not thinking before I spoke, something Jenna usually does when we typically get into trouble. 'I am sorry for your losses.'

"Thank you, and I apologize for the way things turned out, that was not my father's intentions, he hoped for you to be adopted into a loving family that gave you the best care," he replied while staring into the fire.

'It is okay, it wasn't that bad, and if it weren't for that decision, I would not have met my best friend, my sister,' I said while smiling at Jenna who smiled back at me.

"You said she had no memory? How did he, they... How was her memory taken?" Jenna asked, strangely in a sequence of three?

"Honestly, I do not know about that; I never got the chance to learn the truths of it."

Corbin continued to watch the fire, the silence was too much it was unbearable; it was like I could feel his pain because my heart began to ache. I wanted to ask him so many more questions, but my conscious was telling me no not yet, I let him be, but unfortunately, Jenna did not seem to feel or even notice he was in pain as I watched her walk over to him.

"How did they erm, he... well, all of them, how did they?" she said with so much effort, I assume as she got closer and realized what I could see.

'The darkness found us,' he replied.

He didn't go into much detail... well, that was all he said about that. I could see Jenna's lips attempting to move then there was nothing, realizing that it was too much of a touchy subject, so she nodded and stared into the fire. By Corbin's answer and actions, I could sense that he witnessed enough; I could feel him, it was strange. 'What is happening to me?' I thought to myself.

Corbin caught my gaze, "Are you alright, miss Alexa?" he asked.

'Yes.'

"Are you sure?"

Why was he so concerned about how I was feeling? When he was the one that suffered and witnessed a great ordeal, so why was he questioning me?

"Alexa, are you alright? Your head is sweating," Jenna asked, worrisomely walking towards me.

Something was defiantly wrong, so wrapped up in my thoughts I didn't notice that I had shifted my body and my hand was resting on my forehead, and at that moment a delayed reaction indeed, I could feel the sweat beneath my fingertips. I removed my hand; it was clammy and warm. 'Wow, how did I not notice this' I thought.

"It has started, has it not?" Corbin asked.

'Has what started?' Jenna and I said in sync.

"Your abilities."

'Really?' I muttered. 'Look, Corb, let's say for argument sake I believed the no memory, the no mother or father and being born out of nowhere because I was sent from God story, but you expect me to believe that I have powers like some freaking superhero?... I do not think so'.

"Like I explained before, I do not expect one to take in such information, but do not lie, I know you could feel my emotions. I have studied your prophesied life from my adolescence. I know you have always felt out of place, stronger and faster than normal people, at least admit that."

‘There is nothing to admit,’ I whispered, failing to make eye contact as I knew if he looked into my eyes, he would see that I was lying.

“I withdraw my last statement. I do expect you to take this in and accept it; we do not have the luxury of time for your stubbornness and ignorance, my name is Corbin Cathy Michaels, I am the son of the Michaels from the Mary Michaels home of Sanctuary. I was raised and taught about the protector as was my father and his father, and so on. I am the last of my line, and my mission is to guide and protect the protector until they are ready.”

‘Whoa,’ I gasped.

“NO, NO WHOAS, no REALLY, you are Alexandra.”

‘It’s Alexa,’ I cut him off.

“No, it is Alexandra Nemesia. You were given that name for a reason; it describes who you are, the defender of mankind,” he continued, trying to keep his composure.

‘This is stupid.’

“Alexa, come on, don’t be like that,” Jenna intervened.

‘Be like what? This is stupid. I am not a defender; I do not want to be, why me? I did not ask for this,’ I said, trying to control my emotions.

“Your lack of acceptance shows an inner weakness that is not worthy of a defender; you need to accept who you are.”

‘Accept what?’ I shouted back.

“That you are Alexandra Nemesia, the chosen one, our defender, our protector, our only hope for survival.”

I turned my back to him. I didn’t want to hear any more of it. I didn’t even want to look at him, was I behaving disgustingly, rude? Maybe I was, but I didn’t care, I wasn’t going to let this stranger manipulate me anymore. I was a fool for coming here; I wanted to leave. Jenna looked at me; she probably knew what I was thinking of, why she chose to walk over to me.

"Alexa look at me, you know me, I have never believed in any of this kind of stuff, but I believe in you and just think about it, you have never been normal."

'Really, Jenna are you falling for this, this so-called priest, I bet he is not even a real one,' I snapped as I crossed my arms together like a spoilt child who didn't get their way.

Jenna's mouth dropped wide open. From that moment, I could tell she was ashamed of me. Closing her jaw, I watched her take a deep breath, 'you know damn well that was disrespectful, and you are wrong for saying it!!!' she barked at me.

'Just think about it; you have never seemed normal,' she repeated.

'What is normal, anyways?' I interrupted.

"Let me finish," she snapped back. "You have always been different. I have never seen you sick with the flu, cold chicken pox, hmmm no, not one. Never hurt, wait, wait I see you looking at me, hangovers do not count, and okay you have been hurt, but you heal quickly. You have always come across as a leader amongst groups."

'Wait, let me stop you there, when have I been a leader? What groups? I only know you, and last year, I had the flu,' I cut her off, tired of hearing nonsense.

"I obviously mean in the home, you were always the one in control, it was you who strategized the plan that got us out of there, it was you who saved us when we nearly got caught squatting, and you weren't sick last year, I was," she replied.

'Oh yes it was you, but that is beside the point, this is ridiculous.'

"Why is it? Why is this so hard for you to take in? Why is it so hard for you to believe that you are capable of greatness?"

'Whoa, I am rubbing off on Jenna with this sequence of three issues,' I thought.

"Alexandra, listen to your friend, she seems like she knows what she is talking about," Corbin interrupted as he walked over to me.

'It's Alexa,' I snapped back.

"Friend, friend, how I could not see it," he whispered to himself.

"What," Jenna and I said in sync, freaked out by his sudden whispering.

"My apologies, I am mumbling to myself. In the prophecy, it says a protector will be born, through growth, many obstacles will be faced during their journey, and a friend will be gained, a follower. Yes, you are the follower, the encourager, the one who will encourage and help Miss Alexa. Yes, how I didn't see it before. It must have been due to your name; it does not have a meaning, just simple, but that is okay. Miss Alexa, you must listen to the follower, she will help you on this journey."

This man nearly had Jenna on his side; she was even beginning to agree with him, trying to force me to, but that was an epic fail from the moment the word 'follower' left his mouth.

Over the years I have known Jenna, I have seen her only get angry on two occasions, and that was back when we were squatting and nearly got caught, after she was insulted by one of the authorities that found us. Which caused her to lose her temper and let's say her mouth deserved to be washed out with soap, no, bleach, as she told some dirty, disgusting things that day. But that was nothing compared to so many years ago; it was April 1st, 2008. Jenna had just turned 17, and one of the kids from the home, I can't remember her name, but she was picking on her for no reason, calling her names, no wait the previous day Jenna was given a cake as an early surprise.

This vexed the other girl, she hated when the attention was not on her, so self-absorbed, so yes she began to bicker to tick off Jenna, and they eventually started to argue, and I had to diffuse the situation.

Now when I think about it, she was right, I was like a leader amongst the other kids, as I was able to calm the brawl between them. Until the girl made a mistake and called Jenna a follower just because I advised Jenna to walk away, in which she was going to do so she could come with me to our spot to calm down. But that didn't matter, not to miss pissy pants we used to call her. I remember it all now, how could I forget something like that, how could someone be so gorgeous in the face have such lousy hygiene and an ugly personality? She hated us, and we hated her, she would only throw her anger towards Jenna as I was the tallest of the children, and she knew exactly how to push Jenna's buttons. And as she watched Jenna walk away, she muttered, 'My little dog follower' her exact words; it's like it happened yesterday, it still freaks me out to think about it, as this was the first time I realized Jenna had a temper, a hidden storm, I like to call it.

When she said those words, I saw something in her that I had never seen before, the rage boiling in her eyes reminded me of those dramatic cartoons where the eyes would go blood red like the face and steam would be coming out of the head. But that didn't scare the other girl when it should have; she was to blind to see, continuing to chant 'follower, follower,' leading the other kids to join in. When I say that pissed Jenna off so much, she completely lost it and charged into the girl and punched her right in the face. Everyone gasped, shouting 'ooooh' in shock to see someone as small as Jenna knock someone more prominent than her to the floor. Shortly after, a few nuns came to diffuse the situation, shocked and full of disappointment in Jenna's actions, they decided it was best to find her a new home.

Yes, that was their punishment, they were very strict and did not condone violence of any sort, but I wasn't going to let that happen. Every time they had an opportunity to arrange a meeting with other places, I made sure I sabotaged every single one.

Every visit, I told Jenna to act out of character to give the impression that she is too much to handle so the other home would not dare to take her. It worked, a plan that I orchestrated was successful. No one wanted her, well that's what I thought, that's what we both thought until the last visit occurred, the visitors were adamant about taking her. I remember that day, all the details, the way he looked at her and questioned as if he was looking for something. I remember the look in Jenna's eyes as her gaze met mine when the head nun announced that she would be leaving in a week. Terrified, fear, I was never going to see her again, and so from that moment, I made it my mission to get her and myself out of that place for good.

"FOLLOWER, FOLLOWER!!!!" Jenna shouted at Corbin.

"Follower? How dare you.... you know what, Alexa, I don't know what I was thinking, this 'priest' NO this man doesn't have a clue on what he is talking about," she continued as she rolled her eyes, refusing to look at Corbin as if she was disgusted with the way he looked. I was so shocked by her behavior and a little embarrassed, to be honest, especially after the way she bit my head off for the way I spoke to Corbin.

Corbin pissed her off for what he said, but I must admit a part of what he said was correct. Jenna did encourage and help me a lot, why I always call her my rock. She has always supported and gave me advice, and I would listen, so if she feels Corbin doesn't have a clue or is a liar, then I agree, as she is never wrong.

An awkward silence I knew I had to break.

'You have really offended Jenna by calling her a follower, she doesn't favor that word, nor do I.'

"Well, I am just sharing the knowledge that has been given to me, and the unwillingness both of you have to accept the truth is beginning to frustrate me," Corbin replied, muttering the last words.

'Well, I have heard enough, and I am done listening to your lies.'

"Lies," Corbin blurted out loudly, interrupting me.

'Yes, and you have no people skills,' I continued.

"You are right, my apologies, Miss Alexa and my sincerest apologies to you, Miss Jenna, if I truly did offend you. Excuse my behavior. I am not my usual self. You see, I have been on my own for what seems like an eternity. What I have been through and done to find you haunts my soul, I must agree and admit I do lack the appropriate form of communication, the etiquette one requires to perform dialogue, or as you call it, 'people skills.' But what I have shared with you is the truth, I am a priest, I am your protector and guide until you are ready. Miss Jenna, you are the follower. I do not mean it in a malice way; it does not mean you follow and listen. But you are the heart of all that is good; you help the chosen one face the most significant battle against evil, you are the one who will show the chosen one the right way when she is lost, I am sure you have found yourself performing these actions since you have been friends. For whatever reason it is you hate the word follower, I do apologize but deep down, you know I am right, and you believe," said Corbin as he looked into Jenna's eyes.

Jenna seemed like she was being drawn back into Corbin's lies, she didn't say anything, but her silence said enough. Me, on the other hand, I was already getting my stuff together. I couldn't listen to any more of this, I don't know if it was due to shock or me being in denial and not wanting to accept, or something else, but I didn't feel right and needed to leave.

I could feel Corbin watching me and sensed he was about to speak, so I spoke first, silencing him.

'We are leaving.'

"Miss Alexa, please stay, there's still more for you to know," he said, sounding more like he was begging.

Jenna was still silent, watching me, waiting for me to meet her gaze but I did not want to look at those eyes because I knew deep down she agreed with him, and her eyes alone would tell me that.

'Jenna, get your things, we are leaving; it is not safe here,' I muttered as I put on my jacket with my back to her.

Without speaking, Jenna began to get her things and her jacket. I walked towards the door, peeping behind me. I could see Jenna exchanging a look with Corbin before turning her back to him and walking towards the door. I then tried to open the door, forgetting he had a key, 'shit' I thought to myself. Now I have to look at this man and ask to be released after I was trying to leave with a dramatic exit. Sad, yes, I know. But what can I say? I watch too many movies.

'Cough, cough,' clearing my throat, hoping to get his attention, Corbin was already behind me.

"I cannot force you against your will, Miss Alexa, but I will ask you, no I am begging you, stay, I am not the bad guy here."

'I know you're not, I just don't think you are well, and I would like to leave, I am not what you are looking for.'

With that said, Corbin took out his key and opened the door. I let Jenna walk out first and watched on as she disappeared into the tunnel. Just as I was about to follow, Corbin grabbed me by the wrist, his hand shaking.

"Please.... you must, you have to, the world is at stake, mankind is relying on you," he said through his grinding teeth.

'NO,' I shouted back, pulling my arm away from him; so much anger taking over my body, I had never felt like this before. So freaked out, I pushed him back so I could have a head start and bolted down the tunnel to meet Jenna, leaving the crazy man behind.

Running, running, I had finally caught up to Jenna, who was walking ahead towards the exit.

"Alexa, why you...

'Run,' I said, gasping for air and cutting her off.

"Why?" she asked, ignoring my request.

'RUN,' I shouted back and took off ahead of her.

I didn't even give her a chance to ask another question as I took off, but she trusted me, so she followed, we continued running till we passed through the exit. I came to a halt when I realized I had no idea where we were.

"Why did you stop," Jenna said out of breath as she caught up with me. "Actually, why did you start?"

'This way,' I muttered as I started to run again.

Leaving the exit, all I could see were old abandoned buildings surrounding us, nothing about this area looked familiar, I had no idea where Corbin had taken us, that crazy man. What was I thinking going with him, endangering our lives like that? After a few minutes, I started to slow down, running slowly turned to jog then eventually walking, we were walking on the pavement, Jenna was beside me silent. I saw a building across the road, it was tall, red, some of the windows were smashed, and it had a low roof alleyway underneath on the side of the blocked entrance.

'Hey, let us go this way just in case that man tries to follow us,' I instructed Jenna, she nodded.

We started to cross the path. I noticed how quiet it was out here, so dark and abandoned it was beginning to freak me out as I know how this plays out in the horror movies. I was also starting to feel uneasy, but I couldn't let Jenna know, or she would freak out too. We walked over to the alleyway. As we passed the windows, I looked in, nothing but darkness and silence.

"Why were you running?" Jenna asked.

'He grabbed me.'

"What?"

'Corbin, if that is even his real name, he grabbed me, and he was hurting me, so I pushed him and ran.'

"Alexa, are you...

Before she could even finish her sentence, a black car pulled up ahead of us.

"Alexa, is that what I think it is?" Jenna whispered

'I think so. When I signal, I want you to run, okay?'

Jenna nodded slowly. Just as I was about to signal to turn around and run, the doors opened from the car, and two men in black suits stepped out.

'Omg Jenna, it's the men in black, they're real. I knew it,' I whispered to Jenna.

"Really," she muttered under her breath. "Alexa, they are walking towards us, what do we do?"

I looked at Jenna, 'trust me,' I whispered and started to walk towards the men.

The men saw me walking towards them and suddenly stopped, seeing this startled me, making me miss a step and trip on the floor.

'shit'

'Dammit,' I whispered as I started to raise my body slowly, my eyes fixed on my hands, my hands were shaking a little. It was not even due to the fear of running from Corbin or these strangers ahead of me; it was because I had fallen; I had tripped and dropped on the floor. I was so embarrassed I had become the kind of character in the movies that I hated. The ones that always fell down at the dumbest moment in the movies that lead to their death, what did I even trip over just now, air? I looked underneath my knees, trying to see if there was anything there, 'nothing' I thought to myself. I really did trip over air; how stupid I feel...

"Are you alright?" a strange voice asked, interrupting me.

'Yes,' I said as I began to rise slowly off the ground. I looked in front of me and looked at the stranger from toe to head as I rose to my feet. His shoes were black and shiny; they looked new, his trousers, his suit black, smart and looked professionally pressed, fresh as if it had just come out of the store. His face was smooth, no stubble, only clean, he had on black glasses. I couldn't see his eyes; I could not sense his emotions, 'weird' I thought...

'I knew the men in black were real,' I whispered to myself.

"Excuse me?" the man asked, looking at me with a confused expression. I could tell by the way he put his lips.

'I know who you are; you're the men in black,' I said, smiling at him.

The man smiled back at me, “I am sorry, I am not the men in black. I am agent Norman from the FBI, and this is my partner, agent James,” he said, crushing my dreams.

‘Oh.’

“And you are?” he asked.

‘Oh...err I am Alexa, and the girl hiding behind me is Jenna,’ I said, trying to shake Jenna off me, who was hiding behind me, holding onto my arm like a frightened puppy.

“Nice to meet you. It is okay, Jenna, we are federal agents. There is no need to be scared; we are the good guys,” agent James said, trying to reassure Jenna.

“Why are you out here all alone, it is not safe, you are aware of what is happening right now, are you not?”

‘We are,’ I said, trying to meet his gaze through his shades as he continued to stare at Jenna, ‘we were trying to find somewhere safe.’

“Okay, well, here is defiantly not safe. If you come with us, we will take you to a safe place. Well, if that is okay with you?” Agent Norman added.

I looked to Jenna, who was still standing slightly behind but had let go of my arm. I could see worry and fear in her eyes. ‘it will be okay, I promise,’ I whispered to her, she nodded back to me.

‘Okay, we will come with you; you will protect us?’ I asked, which sounded more like a demand.

“Of course, we will take you somewhere safe, where there is more like us, we will keep you safe, Alexa,” Norman replied.

I smiled and nodded at the agent who then walked towards his car with his partner, Jenna and I followed behind.

CHAPTER FIVE

THE STRANGERS – 'FRIEND OR FOE?'

WE FOLLOWED BEHIND the agents as they walked to the car. As we stepped in, both of our doors were shut aggressively by the agents, after, they both walked to the front, opened then climbed and sat in the car in perfect sync. Once their doors closed, each lock slid down instantly around the car, something about that made me feel uneasy, my eyes were stuck on my door, staring, Norman must have noticed the look on my face...

"It is just for extra security, just in case any of those things try to attack."

'Huh?' I muttered.

"The locks. I saw you were staring; I do not want you to feel uncomfortable in any way; this is to keep you safe inside, so you cannot get out... Err, so nothing can get in, okay?" he replied.

I nodded as I looked into his rear-view mirror, trying to meet his eyes, but he still had on his glasses, which seemed strange, considering how dark outside was. I wasn't so keen on these two agents; there was something odd about them, their whole attire looked to new, their cryptic messages within their answers. I don't know; maybe I was over thinking. I wanted to make sure it was just all in my head, and the only way I could do that was by asking Jenna her opinion, but how when the people I wanted to talk about were right in front of me? I looked over to Jenna, who was already staring at me; I could see she didn't feel right about this, either. I just hoped we were both wrong.

"So how did you end up in that place?" Norman asked.

"We...

'As we said before, we were just looking for somewhere safe, we were walking for ages,' I said, cutting off Jenna.

"Oh, I see," said James.

I could feel Jenna looking at me, but I didn't care. I had a gut feeling that something was off with these guys, and I didn't feel up to sharing details about my life with them.

'So how come the FBI is taking care of this? Isn't this kind of stuff for the army?' I asked, surprisingly not in my sequence of three.

"Err, it's anyone available, so many people have turned," Norman answered, staring off into the empty road ahead of us. "Have you come across any survivors?"

'No, just me and Jen. Have you come across any things?'

"When you say things, you mean the taken?"

'Yes, if that is what you want to call them.'

"Yes, we have."

"Why are they, how have they, I don't know what I am asking," Jenna interjected.

"Don't worry, I do. Many others are saying great darkness has corrupted earth; it has been able to poison or let's say possess ones with their darkest nature, impure thoughts, and actions. For example, rapists, murderers, those kinds of people, and only the ones with the purest hearts/souls have been spared."

I could feel Jenna was about to ask another question, so I silenced her by squeezing her hand.

'Can they be cured, brought back?' I asked.

"No"

'How do you kill them then? Is it like zombies and you have to give them a blow to the head?'

"No, it's not like the films, Alexa, they are not zombies but worshippers of the darkness. Any normal way is fine to put them down," Norman replied, almost sounding as if he was defending them because I called them zombies.

Tension had built up within the car like a ball of poisonous smoke entering our bodies one by one, silence between us. I didn't know where to look. Every time I looked into the rear-view mirror, I saw Norman. I could neither tell if his eyes were on the road or directly at me.

When I looked towards Jenna for a while, she just stared out of the window, and after some time, she seemed asleep. 'lucky bitch' I thought as I was so tired, but there was no way in hell I was going to allow myself to sleep when I did not trust these 'agents.' if one sleeps, the other has to take watch just in case shit goes sideways, that was always our motto when we had doubts about anything. Jenna was just lucky enough to fall asleep first. I couldn't be too angry as she did allow me to sleep when we drove with Corbin, I just had to suck it up, watch her back and try to give these men the benefit of the doubt.

An hour had passed, and we were still on the road. The car was filled with silence, no talking, no music, nothing. I was beginning to get annoyed. I was really trying to trust them, but my gut was telling me something else – why are these places so far? Agent Norman could at least try to talk with me to give me an idea of where we were going. Agent James? I was beginning to think he wasn't real; for the past hour, I had not seen him move or breathe...

I couldn't take it anymore; I hated not knowing, so as usual, I broke the silence...

'Where are we going? How long? How far, should I say?' I asked in my sequence.

"Somewhere safe," agent James replied, oh so he is real then.

"Yes somewhere safe, not far, not long to go," agent Norman repeated while answering my other two questions. It was odd and not because of the way he answered, but by the look, he exchanged with James when he repeated somewhere safe. I know they have on glasses, but I defiantly saw a look between them, with their cryptic messages within their answers.

The glasses were beginning to annoy me, seriously, how can one see in the dark with sunglasses. I could barely see out of my window because it was so dark, nothing but silence, not a soul in sight. I gave up trying to see after a while, so it baffled me on why they were wearing them. I had to ask.

'Quick question?'

"Yes, what would you like to know?" asked agent Norman.

I felt Jenna tap me. I must have woken her from all the talking, but oh well she needed to be awake for this just in case anything goes wrong.

'So you're not the men in black, yet you dress like them and wear the glasses like them.'

"Is that a question or statement," agent Norman asked, sounding confused.

'Wait I wasn't done, so why do you wear the glasses? Do you have black eyes? What are you hiding?'

Agent Norman looked at me in the mirror then suddenly stopped the car.

I felt Jenna squeeze my hand, I wanted to signal her to make a run for it, but I remembered quickly that the doors were locked, I tapped her once and mimed it will be okay as I felt her watching me. I looked ahead, staring, no, waiting for his next move. Agent Norman maneuvered himself so we could see his face as did James, they exchanged a quick look then slowly removed their glasses. I watched on, my heart racing, filled with fear, anxiety, waiting for the inevitable, but there was nothing; his eyes were normal. I looked at both of them then, Jenna, her face was just like mine, confused, her hand was clenched so tight around mine. I hadn't noticed before, but she was actually hurting me, but I didn't have time to acknowledge that correctly. I looked back at the agents who were both smiling...

'Huh,' I said so quietly I was practically whispering as I was freaked out, not sure of what was going on. Both of the agents looked back at one another and burst out with laughter... well to me, it seemed like laughter it was kind of creepy in a way like they had never experienced humor before.

'What so...' I said but stopped quickly, still confused and slightly frightened.

"You look lost for words, Alexa, well let me enlighten you; my partner and I saw you from a distance earlier, and we wanted to look cool, so we put on these glasses we found in the car. I found it hilarious when you thought we were the men in black, so I thought it would be a good idea to keep them on, even though if I may be honest, trying to drive and see was so hard, all I wanted to do was take them off," said agent Norman before creepily giggling again.

I looked at Jenna who was already laughing, and I could not help myself but join in too, it was the dumbest things I had ever heard, I thought these men were creepy and off, but in reality, they were just nerdy cops who were trying to impress us. I couldn't stop giggling. Norman turned back around and started the car while still laughing, James continued to watch us while smiling then slowly turned back too, and in that moment we were all equals, no doubts, no cryptic messages, nothing, and I started to feel stupid for doubting them.

"So where are you girls from?" James asked while still smiling.

'We are from the city,' I answered for both of us.

"Oh okay," said James, sounding unsatisfied with my answer. "I have noticed that you seem to do more of the talking, your friend is quiet…do you always take the lead?"

'Err, I do not lead anyone,' I said, sounding defensive, still bothered with what Corbin had shared with me. 'I am doing most of the talking as Jenna's mouth tends to get us into a lot of trouble,' I continued as I grinned at Jenna, who was rolling her eyes.

"Funny," giggled James.

"So you are the troublemaker then," Norman asked.

Jenna didn't answer, continuing to look out the window. I could see the corners of her mouth rising.

"So what did you do before all of this?"

'Well, Jenna worked at a bar, famous for her cocktails and I, well, I was their bouncer,' I answered.

James and Norman exchanged a quick look then looked at me quickly.

"Bouncer?" they both said in sync. "But you are a young woman."

"Yes, but she is 6 foot and stronger than your average human," Jenna interjected.

'Ssssshhhh, Jenna' I silenced her. 'I am not stronger than an average human. How can you say that, have you met the average human? and my sex means nothing, Norman.'

"I am your average human, and I am not as strong as you, and ignore her, she is in denial. I have witnessed her throw huge men out of the bar, like literally pick up off the ground and just throw them," Jenna continued while trying to do the actions with her arms as James watched.

'Jenna shut up, and you are 5 foot, you are not the average human. You are a dwarf, never forget it, and it is quite easy handling someone intoxicated. It's like holding someone in your arms underwater; there is no weight. Shut up, Jenna, stop staring.'

"Ladies, please let's settle down," agent James said, trying to end our debate.

"Fine," we both said as we crossed our arms, staring out our windows.

"Have you always been this strong, Alexa?" asked Norman with a weird look in his eye.

At the moment, I started to feel the doubts resurface; it was like they never left; they were having a break. I began to regret our conversation; I felt like we had shared too much. I started thinking about every question I asked and the answers they had given me, every answer had a deeper meaning, 'somewhere safe,' 'so you cannot get out,' 'worshippers of darkness,' 'we found in the car.'

Oh, my god, this is not his car. He said we found in the car... found???

"Alexa?" Jenna called me, snapping me out of my thoughts, my procrastinating.

"Are you alright?"

'Ye....'

I could barely finish my sentence; my mind was working too quickly, every word, every sentence replaying back over and over, every detail, the suits, the shoes they were two new, and for someone that has already come into paths with the taken, he looked too groomed. These men were lying; they were not who they said they were. They won't even tell me where we were going. The constant questioning our lives, at one point they seemed so interested in Jenna as if they thought she was someone, then quickly shifted their attention and looks on to me.

"Alexandra."

I could feel my gut screaming at me, telling me that something was not right, and now I could hear Jenna call my full name when she knows I do not like when it's called in front of strangers.

"Alexandra."

'What?' I aggressively said as I looked towards Jenna.

"It wasn't me," she whispered.

I looked in front of me. Norman was staring at me through the rear-view mirror.

"Are you okay?"

'Were you just calling my name?' I asked, confused.

"Yes, are you okay. I asked you a question," the agent replied, sounding anxious and annoyed.

'How do you know my name?'

"Excuse me?"

'How do you know my name?' I repeated.

"Is this a joke?" giggled Norman, "you told me your name."

'Yes, I told you my name was Alexa.'

"Yes, is that not what I called you?"

'No, you called me Alexandra, how do you know my name?'

"Oh, my apologies. I meant to say Alexa and by assumption, led me to think it was short for Alexandra, which is a beautiful name by the way," he said. After, there was a slight twitch in his eyes, which at that moment gave it away that he was lying, but I nodded anyway. I did not want them to know that I knew they were frauds.

Norman's eyes went back on the road as he continued driving. I could feel Jenna tapping me; she wasn't fooled by my actions. I grabbed my phone out of my pocket, which luckily still had battery life. I went into my message box and began typing discreetly with my eyes darting back and forth to make sure the agents weren't watching.

I typed into the phone and quickly slid it over to Jenna, the words readout,

'THEY ARE NOT WHAT THEY SEEM; I DO NOT TRUST THEM. WE NEED TO ESCAPE.'

I watched Jenna read as my eyes darted back and forth to the agents. Jenna began typing. I looked away; something wasn't right. I felt weird, not myself, and my vision became blurred. I stared at my hands, they were blurred too, glowing somehow. I felt Jenna tap me as she tried to slide me the phone.

"Alexa, are you alright?" she asked in a worried tone, well what seemed like worried, it was a struggle to make out as her voice echoed repeatedly.

'What is wrong with me,' I whispered to myself.

"Alexandra, are you okay?" I could hear Norman asking.

I looked up to the rear-view mirror; my vision still blurred. Norman's face I could not make it out; it looked disfigured. I rubbed my eyes over and over; my vision was getting clearer. I could see Norman's face, it was just like my drawings, like the taken. I was so shocked I screamed out loud.

The scream was so sudden it caught Norman off guard, causing him to lose control of the car, the wheel was spinning out of control. The car swerved off what seemed like the motorway, causing us to go speeding down the hill into the woods; we were going so fast I held onto Jenna's hand and whispered, 'it will be okay, I promise.'

'Thump.'

The car crashed right into a tree. I felt the impact of my bones hit my chest; I felt an aching pain as my head smashed into the head seat in front of me. My head was screaming, so much sounds echoing around me, the car alarm, the sound of smoke erupting from the bonnet, the sound of the agents opening the car doors with force, the sound of my breathing, Jenna's breath, wait, Jenna....

'Jenna, Jenna, wake up, are you okay?' I screamed as I loosened my belt and moved closer to her. I could hear the sound of the heart beating slowly. I loosened her belt and lifted her head, the left side was bleeding from the collision of the side window, she could have had a concussion, but I didn't care, we didn't have time to rest, so I slapped her across the face.

"Ouch," she said with her eyes still closed, and her head was resting in my hands.

'Are you okay to move?'

"Yea," she said as she opened her eyes slowly. "What the hell was that Alexa, you made the car crash?"

I moved my hand from her head and helped her sit up, 'look we don't have time to point the finger, okay, when we get out of this car I am going to tell you to run.'

"Why?" she cut me off.

'Look, no questions, okay? Trust me, you need to run as fast as you can when I tell you to, and I will be right behind you. I promise, okay?'

Jenna nodded, no questions asked. I took a deep breath and opened the door, which was odd as it was locked before, and quickly stepped out, ignoring that thought then assisted Jenna out onto her feet.

'Remember what I told you?' I said as I stared at her, she looked up and nodded back at me before giving me a brief hug.

I looked around and up to where we came from to see how far the run would be, 'where are they?' I thought to myself, answering my thoughts, I could hear the sound of the staggering footsteps crushing the leaves and branches.

"Are you alright, girls?" Norman asked, covering his face.

‘Stand back. I know what you are!’ I shouted.

“What?” Norman answered in a confused tone but still covering his face.

‘You heard me,’ I said with so much authority in my voice. it was weird I didn’t even speak like this when I was at the bar, but something was taking over me, I didn’t understand it, but I liked it.

“Alexandra, please.”

‘MY NAME IS ALEXA!!!!’ I screamed back, my scream was loud, and it felt so powerful, so much anger within me. As I screamed, every window which belonged to the car shattered to pieces and flew past Jenna and I. Suddenly, a tingling sensation came over me. I was full of energy; it’s hard to explain. I could feel this force traveling through me and around me. I could feel it leave me, but I was still connected to it as it charged towards the agents, knocking them to the ground. I was so amazed but was too determined in getting Jenna to safety to even acknowledge properly what just happened.

‘Run,’ I shouted at Jenna, who was shocked at what she had just witnessed. I was about to scream again, but she had already turned and made a run for it.

I looked back to the agents who were already on their feet...

“Get back here,” agent Norman ordered, before showing his true form. I don’t know why, I don’t know what possessed me, but I stood there, frozen and horrified as I watched... His face and eyes started twitching uncontrollably, and his body began to shake after, his perfect stance, his whole attire was no longer smooth but wrinkled and out of place, he was… The sound of cracking was all I heard next, which I realized after was coming from him, his shoulders were drooped, and his back seemed hunched. His hands, or should I say claws, looked well… it looked like a way overdo manicure and like it should be dipped in bleach for a while, as his nails were pointed and sharp, and the cuticle was black as coal. His face suddenly stopped twitching, but he covered it instantly before I could see anything. I waited patiently as he slowly started to remove his hand.

I wish this were a movie right now so I could forward this shit, I thought. His hand was finally removed, and I could see his face, it looked disfigured, like he had been in a boxing match and lost disgustingly, it was something like that with a cross of being born with a deformity to the face and receiving surgery but the procedure going wrong. No, wait, it's like that film called the mummy, I'm sure you've heard of it, where the mummy is awakened and feeds to generate fully, remember his face? It looked like it had been stepped on, well you get the picture of what I'm trying to say; it was so scary to look at, especially his eyes – they were black as the darkness.

"Get the girl!" he shouted to Agent James, who had shown his true form as well. James started charging towards Jenna, who surprisingly was still close by, watching.

'NOOOO,' I shouted, re-releasing my anger. I could feel it leaving me. 'Run, Jenna,' I shouted out before getting knocked to the ground by Norman, I tried to fight him off, but James joined in too, they were so strong. Norman started to hold me down while James took off again, I could hear her heart racing, her feet picking up speed. I didn't know how I knew or could feel this, but it was driving me crazy. I could feel something taking over me again, anger, fear, all these emotions.

'AHHHHHH!' I screamed out loud, throwing Norman off of me, I could feel the anger, the force beaming out of me, a tornado of wind appeared out of nowhere, picking up the leaves off the ground, they were everywhere. Norman then called out something to James, which seemed to be a different kind of language. James suddenly turned back around and started charging towards me. I closed my eyes and screamed again, pushing my anger more and more. I felt it leave me. I could see it behind my eyelids travel; it was like an invisible entity. It lifted agent Norman and threw him in the air. Norman went flying right into a tree. I heard the crack from his spine as he hit it, his body slid down slowly and smacked the ground, he was dead. James was still charging towards me. I raised my hand to him; my anger threw him back to the direction he came from. He went landing on a big rock, head first. I saw the impact as if it was in slow motion, his head smashing against the rock, the precise moment and sound of his skull cracking, the rock piercing through his brain, the very last pump before his heart stopped, I heard everything. Within seconds, the anger faded and I dropped to the ground… Before I could catch my breath, I heard screams; it was Jenna. I jumped to my feet as fast I could and raced up the hill, but it was too late, the screams got further and further away.

'Jenna, I'm coming. Jenna!' I screamed out, hoping she was okay; I just kept thinking about the last thing I said to her before I told her to run, I told her I would be right behind her. I promised, 'Jenna, please be okay,' I whispered.

I finally reached the top of the hill and entered on to the road. I was too late; the car had already gone a distance, disappearing into the darkness. I began to shake; she was gone, they took her. I had no idea what I was going to do. I was all alone, no car, I was deserted.

I stood there staring into the darkness, a tear rolled down my cheek, and my hands were shaking, I felt so alone and scared. Suddenly, I heard a noise coming from the forest. I was so confused I was sure the agents were dead.

‘Who’s there?’ I shouted out, staring into the path I had come from.

My heart was racing, my palms sweaty, fear, anxiety, exhaustion was all I could feel. I just wanted this moment to be over. The noise got loud then close then closer and closer, and just as I was about to open my mouth to speak, I felt a slight tap on my head. ‘what was that,’ I thought as I raised my hand and stroked behind my head, it felt hot and wet. I quickly moved my hand to investigate it, even in the darkness, I could tell what it was, my hand was covered in blood, and before I knew it, I felt my consciousness slip away....

CHAPTER SIX

TAKEN

'WHERE AM I?'

'Ow my head, my fucking head... shit'...

It's dark; I can't see, I can't see a thing, THUMP, THUMP, THUMP!!! The sound of my heart was all I could hear at first, beating so fast and loud through my chest. I am scared, so scared, struggling to hear and struggling to concentrate on the sound of my surroundings.

Who hit me? Who took me? 'Ssshhh' I stuttered as I mumbled to myself, inhale, exhale, inhale, exhale just like she showed you, I kept repeating, there we go, calm and still as if I was air, no, as if I was non-existent...

I hear something... Is it voices? I can't make it out properly, what are they saying? Where are we going? Are they taking me to where she is? Are they taking me to her...? Jenna...

WAIT!!! I know this, I've seen this moment, this has happened before.

Deja vu? No, this happened in my visions... Oh my god, it is happening, everything she said, everything Corbin said... shit, they were right.

I began to shake, as panic and anxiety took over me. I couldn't believe it, well I did... that was the point. All this running around could have been avoided if I'd just listened, if I'd just believed in myself, we were safe, there was food, water, I wasn't alone. I had my best friend, my sister, with me, supporting me.

I had a chance to know the truth, for questions to be answered finally, that were haunting me all my life. To make sense of all of this bullshit around me, to finally know who the fuck I am, and what did I do? I blew it. I fucking blew it because I was too ignorant, incapable of having an open mind, an ear to listen. Now, look at me sitting in this Mercedes with a bag over my head, two creeps in the front with no sense of emotion, no heartbeat, no humanity. I don't even know how long I was out, how long we've been driving, how far or close we are to Jenna, or where they plan to take me. At this moment, I am a sitting duck, clueless, helpless, alone...

'We have stopped. I know we have, I can feel it', I whispered to myself as my body jerked a little when the car stopped. Come on, Alexa, it's now or never, you need to get away, you've seen this happen already; just let it play out any minute now. I waited and waited, but nothing, no urge to jump out or whatever I did in the vision. This was different; I was calm; I was scared but still calm. In the vision, I was filled with so many emotions. I could feel something in me rising. I don't even understand how I escaped. From what I remember, I flew out the car; there was no door, and my hands were tied. The only way that could make sense if I was in a jeep, but I can't be, there's no breeze against my skin. There wasn't any in the vision either, and I drew a Mercedes in my book. Even though I am having a few doubts about the details from my vision, I can still tell we are not in an open vehicle.

The car started moving again but slowly, and now I can feel everything. I can hear everything; I can see it as I hear it, my mind is projecting an image right in front of me through my eyes. The sound of oil bubbling in the engine, I can see the make and the oil inside, I can hear the needle from the speedometer, 'we are on 30mph' I whispered like I was a militant machine.

How am I doing this? What is happening to me? Am I seriously asking myself questions in a sequence of three?

Snap out of it, Alexa, always thinking, always thinking, it's your fault this happened. You chose to go with the men, you promised Jenna it will be okay, you, you, you...

'Huh? I cut myself off from procrastinating... What was that? What are they saying?' I can't make it out...

"So do we have the right one? OUR LORD WILL BE SO UPSET @&$%%£X."

What, I can understand them, but how can I… oh my god, RIGHT one? Jenna

I can't take this anymore; this is not how the vision was, the crazy dream. Why can't I get this right? I whispered. I began to feel angry inside; I could feel myself boiling up, I could feel the thing inside me that I felt before in the forest returning, the same thing I felt in every dream.

All of a sudden, I could hear the sound of the wind, the trees were blowing, bulbs flickering in what must have been the street lamps passing. Everything around me was speeding up; the oil was getting louder, it smelt hotter, our speed had increased to 50mph, the wind sounded like it was screaming in pain, the lights around us were smashing.

I could hear the creeps; they were making noises, the same noises the agents made as they began to change.

"IT'S HER $%&*@ $%&*@!!"

I heard a voice shout.

I could feel myself panicking. I knew who exactly or should I say what had taken me, it was the taken the irony in that I know I had to get away, but I wanted answers. They had taken Jenna, what if she was dead? I didn't want to think the worst, but I did, and it made me angry, so angry. As my anger increased, I could hear my surroundings more... 'NOW, Alexa'!! My mind then screamed at me, my body boiled over, my heart began to race with such speed then suddenly, 'thump' rolling, rolling, rolling, rolling, rolling then stop. I got up to my feet, the pain I felt in my body was beyond words, but there was no time for that, I had to hurry, and strangely my hands were no longer tied, so I pulled off the bag that was over my head. I looked around; it was so dark, there was barely any working street lamps left, an empty road with trees buried in trees on each side. I could see from a distance the car was turning around coming back for me. I looked down at my legs to check no bones were poking out. They looked fine. They were hurting, but nothing was broken. My arms and hands were covered in grazes and blood. I didn't have time to check anywhere else, so ignoring the pain, I began to run for my life.....

I'm running, I'm running, faster and faster. I've never run so fast in my life I didn't know that I could. What has only been a few minutes has felt like hours, then again, I don't know what's real anymore. Is time itself real? I peeped my head over my shoulder to see how close they were behind me. 'Shit,' I muttered as I noticed how quickly they had caught up, they were getting so close, then closer and closer.

'Thump.'

'Ow,' I screamed as the front of the car hit my leg.

The impact of the blow caused me to stumble out of control, which made me angry, so angry that I sped up and got faster, faster, and faster. I looked back, and the car began to disappear into the night. I couldn't tell if it was from how fast I was going or if they decided to pull back. I could no longer see them, but that didn't stop me. I wasn't going to believe that I am safe and stop running. I hated to see things like that in the movies, the person would be running for their lives and the moment they couldn't see the killer at a distance they would assume that they got away, running would turn into walking, walking would turn to just an abrupt stop then resting somewhere on the sidewalk, then BAM! The killers got you. That shit got me angry...

Well, I wasn't going to end up like them stupid characters with no sense; I kept it moving, well... running to be precise. I made sure to run at least one more mile or a mile and a half to be on the safe side; I am not taking any risks.

I could feel the adrenaline in me slowly wearing off. I was out of breath, still running, well... jogging. I was so thirsty, I was getting tired and wanted to stop, but the truth was, I had no idea where I was, where I was going, and that scared the hell out of me.

'What's that noise?'

From a distance ahead of me, I could hear and see a car coming in my direction at full speed.

'Great, there's more.'

I could feel the adrenaline returning, the anger too. I didn't want to get retaken, but I wasn't running either, my jogging turned to running, and I began charging towards the car with full speed. I could feel myself getting faster. I could feel the force traveling through me, the trees on both sides blowing and moving so aggressively as I passed them, the lights smashing instantly.

I began to scream as I got closer and closer to the car.

The car was an inch away from hitting me but stopped just in time, but that didn't stop me...

'GO AWAY!!!!' I screamed out as loud as I could before slamming down both of my palms on the front, and before I knew, it the headlights shattered into pieces, and the car flew back a foot away from me like something lifted it and threw it away.

'Did I just do that,' I thought to myself as I lifted my hands slowly, looking at them, analyzing them; they were trembling, covered in blood.

I was silent in shock, still staring at my hands, nothing but the sounds of the car alarm flooding my ears.

I could hear the sound of the car door opening, 'leave me alone,' I whispered as I continued to watch my hands shake.

"Miss Alexa," I heard a familiar voice call out.

'Corb,' I whispered back, looking towards the direction of the car which was now hidden in darkness due to the destroyed street lamps and shattered headlights.

"DO not be alarmed, it's me," he said calmly, walking towards me. "Oh my, you're bleeding," he worrisomely said as he got closer, holding a flashlight.

"I must get you to safety right away; I know you don't trust me, but...

'I do,' I said interrupting him, 'you were right. I should have believed you. I am sorry, this is my fault.'

"No, it's not. I am okay, it's not."

'It's my fault Jenna is gone. Jenna's gone, I did this,' I whispered as I continued to stare at my hands.

"It's okay, let me get you to the car and take you somewhere to address those wounds, okay?" Corbin reassuringly said as he guided me to his car.

My eyes still on my hands, no sound, no emotion, no sign in my body language, I just allowed him to guide me.

The drive was slow and silent; I was quiet. If I were to be a computer, I would have a paper stuck to my screen stating out of order, as that was how I was feeling at that moment. No emotion showed on my face, no movement through my body and hands, so still, so quiet. I felt out of order, out of service. I felt out of order within myself, out of order to Corbin, out of order to Jenna...

The only ounce of life in me was my thoughts, which was destroying me inside, images of previous events from the last 48 hours playing back to back.

'You are the defender of the earth.'

'You have never been normal.'

'Stronger.'

'Your unwillingness to accept the truth.'

These are the words my mind continued to scream at me as I thought of the moment I met Corbin. Then the images changed, and all I could see was myself running and running, where was Jenna? Why was I running? I was so confused, but there was no change on my face or in my body language to show the turmoil I was going through.

'It's going to be okay, I promise.'

'It's going to be okay, I promise.'

'The worshippers of the darkness.'

'It's locked so you can't get out... Err, so nothing can get in.'

More words, empty promises that I made to Jenna was all I could think of next. My thinking of running did not last for long; it led me to a blurry film of me walking towards the agents, me promising Jenna something I had no idea I wouldn't be able to keep.

I failed her. I had a bad feeling about these agents the moment we stepped in the car, actually, if I'm being honest, from the moment I saw the suits, the way it was immaculately clean, not a crease in sight as if it had been pulled right from a top expensive suit store.

I could feel something was off about them, yet I still got in the car. I always put our lives in danger; I ignored my instincts.

Reliving these moments were beginning to drain me physically and emotionally, but there was still no change in me, eyes wide open staring out the window, to Corbin it must have seemed like I was staring into the night wondering where we were going, but I wasn't.

From reliving Corbin, to empty promises, to Jenna and understanding the agents, I was afraid what my subconscious would show me next, what my mind would scream out. My mind took me back to running and running again, with voices whispering which I couldn't make out at first, then slowly after I realized it was my voice making the same empty promise.

'It's going to be okay.'

'It's going to be okay.'

The voices got louder and louder, repeating the same promise, shouting then screaming that sounded like Jenna when she got taken, my running was no more. I was still and in front of me were the two agents but no longer immaculate clean and smart, they had transformed into scary monsters, the taken.

A tornado of wind, leaves and twigs with screams was surrounding me, going round and round, it got louder and stronger, I could barely see through it, so I kept rubbing my eyes. Every time I moved my hands, I could see the agents getting closer, I could hear Jenna's screams getting louder, my body was boiling, I could feel it trembling, and my hands were shaking. I was not going to allow these things to intimidate me, so with the screams and wind I let out the biggest roar, and the wind, the leaves, the twigs, the anger all went charging in the direction of the agents.

As I watched on waiting to see the impact of my power collide with the agents, I was left disappointed and confused as I watched it go right through them, 'what' I gasped.

I began to walk over to where the agents were standing, not even realizing the tornado had faded away, there was nothing, no wind, no leaves, no twigs, no them but a dark cloud before me. I waved my hand across the mist to get a better view. as it began to disappear I could see a mirror ahead of me, 'huh' I thought, but before I could even walk closer, I felt my body trembling again, my hands were shaking, and then a sharp pain went right through me.

'OWWWW,' I screamed out.

The pain was excruciating; it was like my bones were breaking, shattering, I couldn't take the suffering. It caused me to lose my step and nearly drop to my feet.

INHALE, EXHALE, INHALE, EXHALE I shouted, gasping for air as I stumbled closer to the mirror. I was nearly there, getting closer. I don't even know why at first I was so keen on getting to it, but now I needed to, I had to see what was going on, why I was feeling all this pain.

I was one step, yes literally one step away from the mirror, and as I was just about to take it, 'crack.'

'Ahhh!'

I screamed as I fell forward to the mirror, which was weird as we were in the middle of the forest and I had just landed on it, and it didn't even fall or move, yet there was nothing it was leaning on, but hey let's not question the unquestionable, this is my subconscious after all.

I backed away from the mirror and stepped back. 'OH MY GOD,' I cried out. I was so shocked with what my eyes could see, it was me well yes obviously it's a mirror, but I didn't want it to be me. My body looked out of place; my hands looked beaten and bruised, my nails, no my claws blood red, my face was fine, a relief, I sighed. But my eyes, my eyes were black like the darkness, like the taken, I was one of the taken…

'Miss Alexa?' a voice called out.

'Alexa!'

"Huh," I said while blinking my eyes repeatedly.

'Hey, are you alright? I thought I lost you there,' the voice replied.

I continued to blink my eyes repeatedly. I could still see myself in the mirror, those black eyes. Every time my eyes closed, I would see darkness then the black eyes again, no idea what was real anymore.

'Alexa,' the voice called again.

Before I could respond, I felt two hands rest on my shoulders; I could feel my body being moved and then suddenly I was being shaken.

"WHAT ARE YOU DOING!!?" I shouted.

The voice ignored me and continued to shake me. I could no longer see the eyes or darkness but a blur then everything became clear, and I could see Corbin in front of me, panic in his eyes as he continued to shake me.

"Hey, hey, you can stop now. I'm okay, Corbin," I said reassuringly as I held onto his arms.

'Oh my apologies, Miss Alexa, you had me really, I can't even use the word, worried. I was flipping petrified, my apologies for my cursing,' said Corbin.

I knew it wasn't the time to be joking around, but really? Is this man seriously apologizing for using the word flipping, is that really a curse word to him?

"I don't understand why you were so petrified," I asked.

'Well, from the moment we got in the car, you have not moved, blinked, breathed, or said a word. I have spoken to you a couple times, but you have not answered. I just assumed you didn't feel like talking,' he replied. 'We have been driving for nearly an hour and nothing. I have even stopped for a bathroom break, and you didn't even move, you just sat there, and I have parked up as we are finally here and I have been calling you and trying to get your attention for over 10 minutes now.' He continued.

"Oh," I mumbled as I looked at him.

'Please, do not scare me like that again, Miss Alexa.'

"I'll try not to; it was not intentional."

'I know it was not I can't imagine what you must have been through since we last met, I was so worried'.

"How did you find me?" I asked.

'I saw you go off with the agents and I went to get my vehicle straight away.'

"But how did you know? How did you know to follow? How did you know we wouldn't be safe? I'm sorry, this is not the sequence. I just don't know what I am trying to ask,' I said.

'I'd be more than happy to share that with you, Miss Alexa, but please let's get you inside and clean you up, okay?' he asked calmly.

I nodded.

'Are you okay to walk? I did see the fall.'

Surprised that he actually witnessed me getting out the car made me eager to get inside so he could share with me what actually happened, 'Yes I'm fine,' I said before getting out the car and shutting it behind me. Corbin sure wasn't lying about me not moving. I felt so stiff from sitting still for so long, but the pain I felt before from the fall was no longer there, 'strange' I thought. I really was in my thoughts on that drive, as I didn't have an idea where we were, it seemed like we were still near the forest of some sort. I didn't recognize anything about this area, and it was still dark, it's actually been dark for a while now.

I walked around the car as Corbin got out, ahead of him was an abandoned old house. It looked creepy and haunted like the type you would see in a horror movie with the stupid horny cheerleader and hotshot boyfriend, and they'd go in and probably play pranks,

I'm not sure, I hated those movies. It's so stupid and unrealistic like someone's really going to go in there when the thing is just screaming out I'm going to kill you with its dirty smashed windows, creaky steps on the patio. The whole house built with tattered wooden planks that used to be beige but is now black, I could go on and on but I will not. The funny thing is I have all this to say about this house, and I'm going into it. I actually feel uneasy about going in there after thinking of the movies.

I could feel Corbin looking at me, "why have you stopped?" he asked.

'I'm not going in there,' I said as I backed away from the creepy house.

"Alexa, trust me, it is safe."

'How do you know that? It's a horror house, a slaughter home, a dump.'

"It is my family home."

'WHAT' I said a little too loudly.

"Ssshhh, not too loud, and yes, I grew up here as a young boy. Believe me, this is the safest place we could be right now. We are too far away, we wouldn't make it back to the other place, especially not with those wounds," he explained.

I still refused to move forward.

Corbin took a massive breath before entering the creepy house, leaving me outside alone. I suppose he wanted to prove a point and check it out for my sake. I stood there for a moment, anxious for his return, but there was nothing, no sound, just silence. I began to feel uneasy, remembering I was in the middle of nowhere, outside a creepy house on my own.

'Corb,' I called out quietly.

'Corbin,' I called out again.

But still nothing. I could feel my heart racing. I didn't want to go in there, but three was no way in hell I was going to continue to wait outside either. So slowly and cautiously, I began to walk to the house, the door was open.

'Crack' went the steps underneath me as I walked to the patio, trying to even out my weight, trying to control my breathing. I walked in and shut the door quietly. As gentle as I was, it still didn't stop the loud click the latch made as the door shut. Quickly, I spun around, ready and alert for anything stupid. As I didn't have no weapons to defend myself, I really didn't have a clue in what I was doing.

Ahead of me was a hallway that leads to god knows where, it was so dark inside I could barely see, so I brushed my hands against the walls to guide me, the texture I could tell was wallpaper, tattered, old. I could tell this place hadn't been looked after for years.

Following the trail of the walls, the hallway came to an end. I could either go right or go left. I decided to take a right, at the end it seemed like a door, so I kept to the wall to guide me and found myself stumbling towards the handle from tripping on who knows what.

'Please, Corb, be okay,' I whispered as I reached for the handle and began turning it but nothing, it was locked, so I turned back around and walked straight over to the other end. As I got closer, still keeping to the wall, I saw a little flicker. I moved closer and realized it was coming from a door. I pushed the door open, causing a loud creak to echo throughout the house. I could feel my heart racing so fast it might as well have been out my chest in my hands beating at the rate it was going.

As I stepped in and got a better look, all I could see was Corbin sitting by a small heater looking up at me.

"What took you so long," he said. "I was beginning to think you weren't coming."

'I thought something happened to you,' I hissed at him, trying to control my composure.

"My apologies but I told you it was safe; you really are stubborn," he replied.

'Thank you, I get it from my parents,' I said sarcastically before slamming the door behind me and charging towards him.

"Relax, I don't want to fight," he said, waving his hands in the air as if he was waving a white flag to surrender.

"Can you just do as I as ask?"

'Fine,' I grunted. 'And what would that be?'

"To just sit."

'What?'

"Sit so I can address your wounds."

'Okay,' I said as I threw myself down on the ground next to the heater.

'But I need something from you,' I asked.

"Anything."

'Tell me everything, my ears and my heart are open. I promise I will listen.'

"Okay, Miss Alexa."

CHAPTER SEVEN

ONCE UPON A TIME WITH CORBIN

I WATCHED AS CORBIN moved the heater at an angle, so it was facing the both of us, but mainly to me. He seemed so concerned about my well-being. I must admit, it felt good to be looked after for once. Don't get me wrong. I love Jenna and being there for her, but this was different, it was lovely.

I watched on as he moved around the room gathering things, yes the room, I wasn't sure if it used to be an old living room or bedroom as there was no fireplace area to confirm or a bed, but there was a back door that probably led to the forest.

A chair with a dusty cloth over it, old beaten furniture scattered in different corners of the room, a wooden chair, and a small wooden square table. The wallpaper looked ancient and dirty with rectangular patches all over the walls paler than the wallpaper around it; you could tell pictures used to lay here.

An old Victorian cloak against one side of the room, those famous tall ones with the ticking and the tocking, except this one made no sound, no movement. I learned after that it wasn't used for the simple purpose of telling time, as I watched Corbin walk over and pull out a key different from the other day, no this key was unique.

He opened the clock and inserted the key into a small hole, the bottom of the clock panel opened, and he pulled out a strange box. Corbin shut the clock back and walked over to me, setting the box onto the table.

"May you rise and take the sofa, Miss Alexa,' he requested.

I nodded and did as he asked.

Corbin pulled over the wooden chair and sat down in front of me so we could be face-to-face.

'What is in there?' I asked.

"You will see," he replied.

Corbin opened the box and started carrying out items – a big bottle of water, tins of food, a first aid kit, a bible, rags, a metal tin.

'Whoa, whoa, wait a minute,' I gasped.

"Is there something wrong?" he asked, looking confused.

'Yes, do you have powers?'

"I beg your pardon?"

'Your box... Is it Narnia?'

"Nar, Nar, I beg your pardon?

'It is a place from a book that I read in the orphanage.'

Corbin continued to stare at me with confusion written over his face.

'You don't know about The Chronicles of Narnia?' I asked, amazed.

"No," he said.

'Wow, so you've never read The Lion, The Witch, and The Wardrobe, not at least one of the chronicles? Well, Narnia is a fantasy world which is discovered by these kids through a wardrobe,' I explained.

"Okay," he said, still confused. "So you think the box is a wardrobe?"

'No, but it is like you keep taking out more and more stuff, where is it all coming from?'

"It is packed really well," he said while giggling, looking into the box. "It was quite a big box, Miss Alexa."

'Hmmm, I must see,' I said as I moved off the chair to get a better look into the box.

I was so amazed by what I saw; there were still many more items he hadn't removed yet, a gun, bullets, blades, vials with strange liquids, a bizarre steel tube.

Corbin watched me as I stared at the gun.

"Like I said before, my family has been waiting for this day for many years."

'Well, actually you said your fathers, father, and his father,' I said with a cheeky smile on my face as I slid back into my chair.

Corbin looked at me with a surprised look on his face.

'Yes, I can remember detail. As much as I tried to ignore what you were saying, I still heard it, and it stuck with me. I have always been good at that kind of thing.'

I said, sounding smugger than before.

“Yes you do, this remembering thing it is one of your abilities, the savior is all-knowing,’ he said.

‘Why do you always talk like that?’ I asked.

“Like what,” he said, sounding offended.

‘You talk, speak so formal, so structured, broken English, I don’t know how to describe it. I can’t get the right words out, but I can feel it’s there. This is more Jenna’s kind of thing, she watches so many types of TV shows, she would know exactly what I am trying to say,’ I said, trying to hold back my frustration.

‘Where are you from? That accent is not, hmmm,’ I paused. ‘Your speech, your posture, you didn’t have a normal childhood, so many rules, so much pressure to be like your father and his ancestors. Your ancestors were originally from England; you were born in England, you’ve been back and forth, that is why your accent is the way it is, proper British, with American trying to break its way through.’

I continued, surprised with myself on what I just shared with Corbin.

Corbin was no longer surprised but impressed with what he heard.

‘Why are you smiling? Was I right?’ I asked.

“I am smiling as I can see a good sense of control; the Savior is all-knowing.”

‘See, there you go again with that, you talk as if you are this magical being, like in the movies the kind that only speaks when answers are needed to save the world or some crazy shit like that, my apologies for swearing,’ I said as I noticed his body language changed.

“Why must you do that?’ he asked with a smirk on his face.

‘What?’

"Speak of your life or things around you and compare it to a movie?"

'I don't always do that,' I said in a defensive tone.

"I never said you did; I just asked why," he said, correcting me in a smug tone.

'Err, I, let's just change the subject, okay?' I said as I had no answer to back myself up.

"Something we both can agree on, Miss Alexa," he said, smiling as he picked up the steel tube.

'What is that?' I said as I watched him move his hand towards the flames of the heater.

"It is an old car lighter, and I am going to rest it in the heater for a while then place it under the metal tin and heat up some water," he replied.

'Okay,' I said as I watched him.

A few minutes had passed, silence between is. I watched as he took out the gun and loaded it before putting it into his bag, as he sharpened each blade and shoved them into a satchel tied to his belt around his waist. The water started to boil; Corbin removed the tin off the tube and reached for a rag and the first aid kit.

"This may sting a little okay," he said as he dipped the rag into the water and squeezed it out, I nodded in response.

Corbin began cleaning my hands first as they were the bloodiest, and after going through three rags, my hands were clean from the blood. I could sense confusion projecting off of him.

'What is it?' I asked.

"I don't understand where the wounds are?" He whispered to himself.

'Wait! What did you just say?' I stuttered.

"Your wounds... your hands, why were they so bloody? Was it even your blood?"

'What, of course, it was my blood, what kind of question is that?' I said, shocked with his accusation.

Corbin didn't respond; he continued to work as if I hadn't even spoken, opening the first aid kit, pulling out a packet of antiseptic wipes and started to wipe my forehead.

"Nothing here it seems," he mumbled.

Corbin sat back in his chair away from me. "Why?"

'I don't know, maybe to have a better look at me...'

"How are you feeling, Miss Alexa?" he asked in a freakishly weird tone.

'What, do you mean emotionally?' I asked, confused.

"No. I mean physically, I saw that fall. I saw how fast the car was going and how far you rolled down the road. You should have suffered serious injuries."

'What do you mean I should have suffered serious injuries?'

"Well, I've cleaned your hands and underneath. Your hands are fine now; how do they feel? Your head and face were covered in scratches and blood, but now, it's like it was never there. So, I ask you again; how are you feeling, Miss Alexa?"

'Well, I actually feel fine. I felt a little stiff when I got out of the car from sitting for so long, but I'm okay now. My hands feel fine,' I said as I looked at them.

'My head doesn't hurt, my legs were aching, but now, they are as good as new,' I said as I moved my legs back and forth. 'What does this all mean?' I asked.

"Hmmm, fascinating," he said as he held his hand on his chin. "I have a thought," he continued as he sat forward and began digging through his bag.

"Aah… here it is," he said, smiling as he pulled out a thick, black, mysterious book.

Corbin started flicking through the pages. "Ah, where are you? Yes, here we are, 'And the Angels waited in fear as a great evil came upon the earth; all but one will be safe,'" he said. 'There is a plan, a Savior.

The Savior will protect.

The Savior will save many.

Gifted with the powers of God.

The Savior is Omniscient – all-knowing

The Savior is Omnipotent – unlimited power, controlling all elements.

The Savior is Omnipresence – everywhere.

Immortal – Can feel harm but will heal quickly.

'Wait, wait,' I cut him off practically whispering. 'I'm like a god? I…I…I can't die?' I asked.

"No, I suppose not," Corbin replied, sounding like he was as confused and shocked as much as I was.

This was all too much to take in for the both of us. Corbin's reaction to it all made it very clear that he only just started believing in this stuff, but I decided to change the subject to lighten the mood.

'So, was I right before? About your family and where you lived?'

"Yes," he said quickly and bluntly, shutting down that topic. I don't think he meant to as I could sense pain from him after. I know he didn't want to talk about his past, but he said he would tell me everything.

“What would you like to know, Miss Alexa?” he asked, with his eyes piercing at me.

‘You said before that you saw the fall, but how? Because you weren’t near me.’

“Well, when I saw you and Miss Jenna get in the car with those agents, I knew something was off, and even though you didn’t believe me and I let you leave, I must guide and protect the Savior until they are ready, so I followed you.”

‘Really?’

“Yes, I was following you. I actually lost you at one point till I heard the screams and I found you again. I was hiding in the forest when I saw your body being dumped into the car, so I ran back to my vehicle and kept a distance from the taken. The funny thing about disgusting, mindless creatures is that they are very paranoid and smart; that’s why I had to keep such a distance tracking you.”

‘So, how did you see the fall if you were so far away?’

“You see this,” Corbin said as he pointed at a weirdly shaped pole he removed from his bag.

‘What is it?’ I asked, confused.

“It is a bino-telescope. I’m not going to bore you with the name; it took me 3 weeks to learn how to pronounce it, but it’s something I came across during my visit to Egypt. I know you think it doesn’t look like an ordinary telescope. Well, you’re right because it’s not; this beautiful artifact was recovered in 1856.”

‘Corb, please!’ I cut him off.

“Right. I’m waffling, aren’t I? Well, it allows you to seek objects from far, in the night, in the light, in the sky, below the dirt”.

‘So, is that how you found me?’ I asked, intrigued.

“No, Alexa, it’s just bino-telescope,” he said while rolling his eyes.

'Sure. Anyways, can you tell me how I escaped from the taken?'

"Yes."

There was a brief silence between us.

"Oh, right. You mean now; well, the car was moving at full speed, the trees were moving uncontrollably around you, then suddenly, the passenger door just… I don't know, it flew off, but didn't fly off. It's like it was ripped off and went flying into the forest. Then you hovered out, and the tie around your hand disintegrated, and you were suddenly on the floor rolling.

'I hovered,' I said, not sure of what he meant. 'I flew.'

"Well, yes if you want to put it that way. Yes, you didn't jump out; you were floating, if that makes more sense to you," he said.

'Okay, then what happened next?' I asked this, trying to absorb what he had just shared.

"I jumped back in my car and started to drive towards you."

"Is there anything else you would like to know regarding this matter?" he asked in a keen tone.

'No,' I said.

Five minutes had passed and I was still silent, "Alexa, are you okay? Are you ready to ask more questions?"

'Yes, sorry! Alright, let's start; who are you, why did you choose this life?'

"Okay, I'll start from the beginning. I was born April 16th, 1975 in London, England; Westminster, to be precise. I lived and was raised there to the age of four, we then moved to America."

'Why did you move?' I asked, interrupting him.

"My father felt that over the decades, the church that we were living in lost its way. He was a traditional man, and he had been a part of many communities amongst the Catholic people, and he could no longer bear to be around the Methodists. It made him realize what he wanted to be, and how he would do things, so we moved to Washington, where he trained to be a priest at the Wesley Theological Seminary. My father was a stubborn and arrogant man; he didn't want to be a full Catholic priest as they cannot be married. He didn't favor the Methodists either, but with them, he could still have his family. So he stuck with them to learn and gain what he required. Once he became a fully-fledged priest, he and other believers formed his own community, the Mary Michaels Sanctuary,

'Mary?' I interrupted.

"Yes, Mary, my mother," he replied.

'I've noticed you haven't said much about her, why is that?' I asked.

"Because she is dead," he said sternly.

'Oh, my God! I am so sorry, Corb. I had no idea even with this omniscient ability,' I said trying to hold back the emotions my body was now flooded with.

"It is okay, Miss Alexa. She passed away a very long time ago, and your power is not at its full peak yet or controllable, so you won't know everything yet,' he replied as I squeezed his hand.

'When did she die?' I asked, completely disregarding his comment about my power.

"I was nine years of age when my mother passed, I still remember that day… They said it to be cancer at first.

'They?'

"Doctors, priests, but not my father, tests after tests, specialists, but nothing; not one person could figure out what was wrong with her. They thought it to be cancer at first because of the way she got so sick and weak. But my father knew what it was, and he knew there was nothing he could do to save her. It was torture for him to see her suffer as it did I, but she was so strong, always smiling even in her last moments".

'Corbin, I am so sorry, I truly am.'

"Really, it is okay Alexa, I'm okay."

'You said your father knew... what it was? How? What was it?'

"He knew it wasn't something that could be explained by science. Shortly after we moved to Washington and my father was training, networking with other communities to prepare for the Savior, he noticed things around him. He told me once that he could sense a dark presence coming, it was close by, and it wanted to stop our mission. He believed it got to my mother, it made her sick, and it made her feel pain then killed her. Shortly after her death, he completed his training and formed the Mary Michaels Sanctuary in respect to her; he made a promise to himself that he would keep searching, preparing and fighting for her".

'What was she like, Corb?' I asked as I leaned forward to hold his hand.

"To be honest, I don't remember much, but I could never forget her eyes; they were blue and always so sincere. I remember the smell of her dark hair, it smelt like jasmine and vanilla, but that's it; I have no pictures, just those faded memories and stories from my father. She was as passionate as he was about being ready for the savior's arrival; she was his rock."

'I wish I met her, Corb.'

"Me too," he said as he squeezed my hand tightly.

Corbin picked up the car lighter and faced it towards the heater again.

'What are you doing now?' I asked curiously.

“I’m going to heat up a tin. I don’t know what your desires are, but I am completely famished,” he said while he rubbed his belly smiling.

‘Oh, I see. Could you heat me up one, too, please?’ I said, smiling back.

Corbin nodded as he picked up the lighter and rested it underneath the tin.

‘Can I ask you a question?’ I asked.

“Of course!”

‘I remember you said before when you were explaining why I was sent away, that it was because the darkness had found you, what did you mean by that?’

“Here you go,” he said as he passed me the tin and a spoon. “Miss Alexa, I would like to apologize,” said Corbin.

‘Apologize for what?’ I said, with my mouth full of- I have no idea what it was, but at that moment, I was starving, and I would have eaten wood to settle this hunger I had been ignoring.

“I haven’t been frank with you, just let me finish,” he said, like he knew I was about to talk. “I haven’t been honest; as in, I wasn’t an only child. Yes, you are looking at me like, ‘why would I not mention that?’ Well, let me explain, Alexa. I have a brother, an older brother.”

‘What?’ I blurted out, nearly choking on my food.

“Yes, I am sorry for not sharing it with you, but it is only because I was ashamed.”

‘Why would you be ashamed, Corb?’

“Remember I said the darkness found us? Well, he is the darkness; he was older but only by a year and 6 months. We were inseparable, we did everything together, but when my mother died, something died in him too. It's like he died that day with her and something else stayed behind. He was never the same as Michael again."

'Wait a minute,' I said, cutting him off trying to hold back my laughter. 'Your brother's name is Michael, as in Michael Michaels?' I said, bursting out with laughter.

"Yes, my brother's name is Michael. Well, I can say our parents weren't that creative when it came to name giving. You think I didn't see the looks you and Miss Jenna exchanged when I told you my name and my middle name, Cathy?" he said with a smirk on his face.

I couldn't help myself; I completely forgot about his middle name and hearing it again led me to a burst out laughing again.

"Yes, laugh it up, Miss Alexa; let it out. My mother was not a cruel woman; I know she loved me dearly as I do her, but I realized she desired a daughter. I surprised her, so she and father thought it would be fun to name me Cathy; I was her secret 'princess,'" he said while rolling his eyes.

My laughter got louder, and my smile got bigger.

'I'm so sorry, Corb,' I said, trying to calm myself down, 'that is the funniest thing I've ever heard, but back to err… I am sorry, I can't call him that name; it's going to throw me off. Hmmm, yes, so about mickey, what do you mean he wasn't the same?'

"He started to change; he became sinister and began to make up excuses not to go to church. He stopped saying prayers at the table, then one day, he just came straight out with it that he does not want to go to church. I remember it so well; he was only sixteen, and my father asked him if he had lost his faith.

'What happened to him?'

"It was his eighteenth birthday. We prepared a meal for him; we were seated at the table waiting for his arrival. He knew he had to be home by 6, but he never showed. My brother was 10 when my mother died, and as he got older, he started gallivanting with the wrong crowd, doing things that he shouldn't. When he didn't show up for the meal, my father was furious. At the time, I don't think my father realized it was the darkness. I think he assumed it was adolescence; a phase, but that night changed everything, as it opened his eyes to the truth. Deep down, I knew the truth; I knew that wasn't my brother, I just didn't want to accept it, but the truth was the moment my mother died, he died too. After the funeral, my brother scared the hell out of me and as the years went by, I kept my distance and made sure not to get in his way. And every night I prayed and begged my God that my brother would spare my life and not kill me in my sleep."

'Wow! That is terrible, Corb. So, what happened that night?' I asked.

"Well, my father had an idea where he would be, so we went after him. He was at this bar, but not an ordinary one; the people there were creepy. I had seen this bar before but never been inside, so I assumed it was a regular bar as did my father. But when he walked inside and even with what he saw, his eyes weren't open till he found my brother and they argued. I remember the constant yelling back and forth after my father managed to drag him outside, then Michael showed us how he really felt, and once again, my father, shocked and hurt, asked him if he lost his faith. As soon as he said that, Michael started to laugh uncontrollably and repeated 'no son of man, no son of God. I worship darkness, that is my god.' He continued ranting on, saying he believes in god, but he hates him, and god is a coward, and once the earth is taken over, he is coming for him. He will be coming to destroy us all when the ruler arrives.'

'Corb, I don't know what to say,' I said as I watched him sit back and eat his food which must have been lukewarm by now. 'Err, so what happened to him? Did he get sick as the same darkness that was in him was in your mum, right?'

Corbin gulped down some of the water, then cleared his throat.

"After that night, we never saw Michael again. Sorry I can't call that thing Mickey,' he said while winking at me. "As in sick, I believe it made my mother ill because she was pure, and she fought it back. Michael was younger, stronger but not strong-willed, so it was easier for it to take over. I have never seen him again since that day."

'But you said the darkness had found you,' I added.

"Yes, but I wasn't clear in that; I wasn't there. After that night, I went off to college in England. I hadn't lost my way or faith, but my father agreed that it was best to get away for a while to live my life for a bit."

'So you weren't around when they found me?' I asked.

"No," he said. "I was in England when they found you. He sent me pictures, and you were so small and beautiful but looked so mature for your age."

'Age?' I said confusedly. 'I thought you said that they raised me and trained me?'

"They did for two years when you were first born. You were a baby for a few days when you were found; you were a toddler; when you arrived, you were four years old with the mindset of an adult, because you spoke perfectly.

'So let me get this straight; I was ageing rapidly, and you still sent me to an orphanage. How did you know I weren't going to age then? How come I stopped ageing so quickly? Why am I not ageing rapidly now?' I asked in my sequence of three.

"Oh, fascinating. Felt like it has been decades since you've asked questions in that way," said Corbin with a big fat grin on his face.

'Please,' I said, trying not to grind my teeth.

"They didn't know if you would age, but they didn't have a choice. You were so close to being found; they had to take that risk, and from the two years they were with you, you seemed to be ageing normally. I believe they thought maybe because you were around them, your ageing slowed, and when you went to the orphanage as you were around other children, you adapted to them. You have adapted to us; you understand and now have humanity, something my father wanted for you. It was my brother who was coming for you, Alexa; he managed to corrupt people around us to get answers. When I got word of his plans, I got the next flight from England to assist in your safety, but when I arrived, it was too late; you were already gone. My father put your care with a man he trusted, his best friend, James Myer. My father told me that day James left he never saw him or you again, we searched for you for a while but left it to hope that you were with a loving family. On your 18th birthday, you were supposed to regain your memories and return to us to continue your training, but you never returned, and we have been praying for your return ever since".

'Why didn't you search for me?' I asked, intrigued, wanting to learn more.

"My father was a traditional man who believed in his faith; he relied on it, and believed God would return you to us when the time was right. I, on the other hand, completed my training after you disappeared, and became a priest by the age of 26. Then I went travelling to locate more resources for your arrival. Well, that's what I made them believe, but I really was looking for you. I thought James turned to the darkness and had you locked up all these years. I've done some terrible things over the years looking for you; I am not proud of them."

'So, when did you realize I wasn't taken?' I asked.

"Two months ago when the taken arrived at our sanctuary and slaughtered everyone around me, my brothers doing!" he replied as he looked onto the fire of the heater.

'I asked you before about being a priest, and you said it was complicated, when did you lose your faith?'

"When a young boy had become one of the taken, slit my father's throat right in front of me, and I had to take his life," he said before breaking down crying with his head in his hands.

'Jesus Christ! Oh, Corb,' I spit out before leaning to comfort him. 'I am sorry, I am so sorry I doubted you, I am sorry I don't remember; I wish I did, so I could have been there to save them, but you know what? I am here now and I'm ready to accept who I am; I am ready to learn and be who I always was.'

"Bless you, Miss Alexa," he said as he quickly sat up to fix his posture. "We must prepare at once; acceptance is the first step, and it's the key to your power. It will be amplified soon at its peak, and we need to work on controlling it, okay?"

Corbin was sitting upright again; you would have never known he had just broken down just now, he looked very calm.

Just as I was about to speak.

"Ssshhh," he said as he put his finger towards my mouth.

“Do you hear that?” he whispered.

‘Hear what?’ I whispered back.

And before I knew it, the door that led to the hallway went crashing down with bodies on it and the taken stumbling through.

‘Corb,’ I cried.

‘It’s the taken; we must leave at once,” he shouted before throwing the rest of the contents of the box into his bag.

I continued to watch the group of taken struggle to get through the door; I was frozen with fear.

“ALEXA, BACK DOOR! RUN NOW!” Corbin shouted at me while grabbing my shoulders.

CHAPTER EIGHT

GREAT HERE COMES THE TAKEN!

'DON'T YOU EVER do that to me again,' I shouted at Corbin as we ran into the forest.

My heart was pounding aggressively through my chest, trying to keep up with Corbin; my mind showing me flashbacks of the last five minutes.

It terrified me watching on as Corbin ran back into the house, leaving me alone; a feeling of fear taken over as I waited there silently. The sound of furniture being tossed about, the sound of a struggle between Corbin trying to fight off the taken. I really thought he was dead at one point from the noises echoing from the house, but no, this fool was fine. I came to realize that when he bolted out the door running past me and looking back to scream out 'RUN.'

"I apologize, Miss Alexa, but I required something," he said as his running came to a halt.

'What is it?' I said, stopping behind him.

Corbin turned around to face me; in his hand was a silver fixture.

He moved closer, took my hand, and dropped the silver fixture in it.

'It's a...

"Cross," he said, finishing my sentence.

'Are you kidding me, you risked your life for a cross? And why is it so heavy?' I barked at him before dashing the cross back in his hands.

"Ssssshhhh... The plan has worked; they are following us," he whispered.

Corbin's plan was to lead the taken away from the house into the forest to the motorway, so we could double back to the house and get to the car and break free. It seemed like a simple task, but I don't think even Corbin expected what was about to happen next. We were running again, and Corb was ahead of me.

"Keep running, Alexa," Corbin shouted back at me.

'I am trying,' I said, gasping for air, so tired and out of breath, which was a mystery to me on why I was so tired after how fast I ran before.

I could hear the taken behind me; they seemed so close. I had to see; I just needed to see, so I peeked over my shoulder, and as I did, there was a deformed man an inch away from me.

Before I could even scream, all I heard was a loud bang, then something went right through his head, and a spec of blood flew on me; the man went crashing down on the floor causing others to trip over him. I turned my head and in front was Corbin holding a gun;

he kept at his hand and pulled me to run faster as he started firing at the taken. I was so shocked…thinking what kind of priest was he? I looked back again while he shot; he was actually a good shooter. I watched as the bullets fired taking down one Taken at a time, some Taken went crazy and started speeding up and just as Corbin was about to shoot one, it dodged the bullet and ran up a tree.

'Oh, shit! Jenna wasn't kidding about these things,' I whispered. Feeling guilty for ever doubting her too, we really needed to hurry and get out of this forest. I must find her, I will…

I couldn't look anywhere; I was too scared, so I kept my eyes on the target- the path to the motorway. Corbin kept running and shooting, and I was his eyes, but as we reached the edge of the forest that takes us to the road, I froze.

"What are you doing?" he said as he turned to look at me.

I didn't speak; I just lifted up my hand and pointed towards the road.

"What?" he demanded and a second after his eyes followed my hand, and he indeed was shocked and frozen with fear. Ahead of us into the road was the Taken standing in a line horizontally. Corbin's face was serious, beads of sweat dripping down from his head, his hand gripping tightly on to his gun and cross; he looked behind us, the Taken were also standing lined up and waiting.

"Stay by my side," he whispered through his teeth.

I nodded.

Corbin and I began strolling into the road towards the Taken.

He stopped as we were entirely out of the forest but an equal distance from both of the Taken in the forest and the road.

"Is there something you require?" Corbin shouted, but there was nothing but silence between them and us. "You will answer me, God dammit!" Corbin shouted again with so much anger and authority I could feel it beaming off him.

The Taken still remained silent.

"Very well," Corbin whispered to himself while loading his gun.

'Give us the girl," they all said in sync as one.

"Never!" Corbin hissed back at them.

'Give us the girl or die,' they repeated again as one.

Corbin didn't respond; instead, he looked over to me.

"Here, I want you to take this," he said as he handed the gun to me. "The safety is here, you release and press this when you need to shoot," he explained as he showed me the gun.

He then took off his bag and put it on me.

"Everything you need to know is in the book, you have supplies, and the car keys are in the front. When I tell you to run, you need to get the hell out of here as quickly as you can."

I didn't respond to him or nod, I just looked into his eyes while mine filed with tears like a frightened, little girl staring at her father as he walks off into war.

"It was a pleasure knowing you; an absolute honor, Alexa," he said emphasizing my name at the end to show he left out the miss. "I believe in you, now it's time to believe in yourself," he said before kissing me on my forehead.

'Give us the girl,' they repeated again louder than before.

"You get ready," he whispered.

I looked at Corbin and began walking around him towards the direction I had to run.

'Get the girl,' the Taken shouted together before breaking out to attack.

"RUN!" Corbin ordered as he held onto his cross.

I began to take off tears running down my face, I couldn't believe this was happening; I didn't want it to, especially the fact that this man was risking his life for me, no scarifying and he gave me everything so he can keep a useless cross for himself. No, I won't do this, I won't leave him. I turned around ready to help Corbin to see him still holding the cross praying out loud, the Taken were slowing down around him.

'Oh, my god! It's working,' I thought, but I was wrong.

The Taken stopped moving; they were perfectly still, then one broke out laughing, followed by another and another.

"Very well then," Corbin shouted out before holding out his cross.

I watched closely as his finger pressed the center, the cross then extended into a sword.

'No freaking way,' I whispered.

Corbin held the sword up into the air. If this was a movie, this would have been one of those frozen scenes just before a big fight is about to happen; the enemy's faces as they stare at the weapon the intensity between all of them. Corbin let out a roar as did the Taken as they all went charging towards each other, but that didn't scare him I could feel it, Corbin moved quickly maneuvering the sword stabbing, slicing, ducking and flipping while reciting a pray out loud.

I was so amazed; he was like a freaking hitman. His moves were so precise, so smooth, so fast nothing could stop him. Well, at least that's what I thought at that moment.

I was wrong; there were too many of them, Corbin had the upper hand for a moment then more Taken came charging out of the forest.

‘Corbin,’ I screamed out scared for his life.

Corbin caught sight of me, and in that second I was a distraction, as his eyes were on mine. The Taken managed to disarm him and knocked him down to the ground.

“Alexa, no, run!” he yelled out from the floor as they began kicking and beating him to death.

Some of the Taken noticed me coming and began charging towards me; I remembered the gun in my hand and started to fire, which was a flop as I forgot the safety was on.

‘Aah,’ I screamed as I struggled to work the gun, leading me to toss it out of anger.

I could see Corbin trying to break free from the Taken, suddenly each of them began to shake uncontrollably, their mouths began to water, and they were getting ready to feed.

‘No, Corbin,’ I thought. I could not let this happen after everything we have been through; after everything we have shared with each other. He is my friend, my family. I could feel the anger in me rising, I could feel my speed picking up, and I could hear the sound of Corbin’s heartbeat as he continued to try to defend himself from the ground.

The Taken that was charging towards me was getting closer. I continued to run towards it, and one got close enough to grab me. I screamed, grabbing its wrist, then twisted and threw it into a tree. I could feel myself getting stronger, I clenched my fists as hard as I could and threw my fists into the next thing in my way.

More and more Taken came charging towards me, leaving him alone, then I had an epiphany; I understood who I was now, I knew what I had to do. Suddenly my body started to feel weird – light, if that makes sense. I was no longer running, I was walking, but inside

I felt like I was floating. I looked at my hands, they had a white glow around them as did my arms. I stopped for a second, looking at my hands, the Taken ahead looked as if they had been slowed down, slow motion. The Taken leader of the bunch moved his lips slowly as he looked towards a beaten Corbin, saying FEED!

Instantly, time was no longer slow. I had reached breaking point; there was no way in hell, in heaven, on earth that anyone was going to hurt my family.

Inside me, a bomb had just gone off and I was on fire internally and externally,

"Get her!" the voice instructed.

My eyes bypassed each Taken as they charged towards me and on to the three that were just about to feed on Corbin. I screamed out as I let my power hit all three of them, causing them to let out moans of pain as they jumped up into balls of flame.

My concentration interrupted by a fellow Taken in front of me attempting to tackle me to the ground but were blasted away by my power around my glow of white light.

My eyes led back to Corb as he laid there on the ground beaten but not defeated; a wave of relief and love flowing from him. Proud that I finally became who I always was, the Savior.

'I am who I am,' I recited to myself then closed my eyes and let out a deep breath as I felt the fire surrounding my body leave me and hit everyone around me except Corbin, of course. The sounds of the Taken were all I could hear; loud roaring, moans between them and bodies twitching in and out of place.

'This was taking too long,' I thought to myself. These things were not people anymore, yet it was still unbearable to watch. I took a few steps closer slowly rising my arms; I didn't really know what I was doing, but I did if that makes sense. I just gave my body, my mind and my heart to the power within me to take over.

Opening my arms slowly as I watched the Taken burn. 'Now rest,' I whispered so quietly and slowly that if I were being watched on TV, you would have never noticed me speak. I pressed my hands together as if I were about to pray, then lowered them looking at the Taken one by one through my eyes and through theirs. I repeated 'now rest' as each one turned to ash, hitting the ground. Once the last of the Taken had fallen, I could feel the glow of fire around me beginning to fade; I could feel the boil inside me going flat. I was calm until I looked over to Corbin laying there sensing his life slip away.

'Corb,' I whispered and within a second from standing a yard away from him, I was right in front dropping to my knees.

'Corbin,' I cried out.

"Alexa you did it; I knew you could," he blurted out struggling to breathe.

'Don't talk, okay? You're going to be okay,' I said, trying to hold back my tears as I looked unto a beaten, bloody Corbin.

'It's going to be okay, I promise,' I said as I rolled him onto his back correctly and straightened out his body.

'It's going to be okay, I promise,' I repeated and repeated as I rocked back and forth on my knees with my right hand on his head and my left on his chest, onto his heart.

'It's going to be okay, I promise,' I said one last time as I watched him close his eyes as I did mine. Tears rolled down my cheeks as my eyes remained closed; I could still hear him breathing and feel his emotions, then suddenly nothing. No slowdown of the heart rate for me to say, yeah, he's dead. Everything just vanished I couldn't sense a thing.

I stayed for five minutes holding on to his head and heart, my mind screaming at me to concentrate.

'You can do this, Alexa!'

'You can't screw this up.'

'You need to focus.'

'Concentrate!'

After a while, I sat right next to him waiting for something, anything, and truth be told, I was too scared to get up and leave; I didn't even know where to begin without him. Half an hour had passed and I still couldn't sense anything, was he really gone?

I felt so alone, my emotions came crashing down. I began to sob right in my lap, then suddenly, I heard the sound of Corbin catching his breath.

'Corb?' I cried out, lifting my head out of my lap.

"What happened?" he asked, still lying on his back as he looked up right into me. "Why are you crying?"

'I thought you were dead,' I said, wiping away my tears, 'you were dying, and I tried to save you, then I couldn't feel your life anymore. You've been out for nearly 45 minutes, but I can sense you now, thankfully. How do you feel?'

"Well, I don't know," he said, sounding not sure of himself as he tried to sit up. "I actually feel great," he said as he moved his arms and clenched his fists that were covered in blood.

Corbin got to his feet and started bending his legs and clicking his neck, side to side.

"Goodness gracious, I feel amazing. I don't have that funny click in my shoulder anymore, and you've healed me," he said, sounding more like a declaration than a suggestion. "Bless you, Miss. I mean Alexa, thank you," he said as he held on to my hands, "oh my apologies for the blood," he said quickly as he removed his hands from mine.

Corbin looked a mess, his torn clothes, bloody face and nose, but if I really did help him and he healed like I did, then I knew that this was old blood and it needed to be washed off, so I looked for the bag to get the remaining water, but it wasn't there.

"What are you looking for?" Corbin asked, watching me confusedly.

'The bag you gave to me; I don't see it,' I replied.

Corbin looked at me, then looked around and started smiling.

'What?' I asked.

"It is over there by the grass leading to the forest."

'How? I didn't take it off. I don't even remember,' I said confused.

"Yes, before you went all glowy, you threw it to the side."

'I did? How strange I don't remember; I do remember the other stuff. Wait, glowy, you saw that?'

"Yes, you would as that was your first real-time harnessing your power. Things will be cloudy at first, and yes, glowy, well, a walking flame to be precise and your eyes were snow white," he said as he walked over to the bag and pulled out the bottle of water.

'Wait, I have snow white's eyes?' I asked with so much enthusiasm than I should have.

"Who?" Corbin asked confusedly as he poured the water over his hands and face.

'Really, Corb, you don't know about Snow White? Didn't you ever read a book when you were a child?' I said, irritated.

"I did, just not those of that kind," he said as he dried off his face when he removed the towel. I saw his face, and I saw that I was right about the blood; it was old, and he was fully healed. He looked brand-new, even his dark rings and bags were gone.

Corbin put the bottle back in the bag then walked back over to where he laid and picked up his sword, then pressed the button and pushed it back into the cross it was before.

'Wow, I had no idea it was.'

"Yes, I know," he said, cutting me off.

'I was so scared when they came charging towards you, but it was so cool when you pulled out the sword. I was like, whoa! What kind of priest is he?' I said, smiling at him as we began walking to the car.

'Well, it explains why it is so dense. Where did you get it from, and where did you learn to fight like that?

"My father gave it to me as did his father and son and other generations, and I have travelled all over the world studying different cultures," he replied, smiling back at me, not trying to sound big-headed.

It was quite a far walk back to the car, I didn't realize how far we had run, so I took the book out of the bag – the mysterious black one, and began flicking through the pages. As I flicked through each page scamming and remembering without realizing, it made me remember something.

'Oh, shit! I mean, err… sorry,' I blurted out, trying to correct myself.

"It is fine, really it is. Stop looking at me like that," he said as my eyes pierced at him. I must have looked frightened and shameful.

"What is the problem, Alexa?" He asked.

'I just realized I don't have my bag,' I replied as I looked ahead of us into the night.

"Bag?"

'Yes, my personal things are in there, and the last remaining sketchbook. I need it, Corb; there could be important information in there.'

"Okay, very well. We must see the bag, but where does the bag rest?"

'Seriously, Corb, you're my friend, no, my family.'

"Family," he said, cutting me off sounding shocked and excited. I could see it had touched him.

'Yes, family,' I continued. 'We have been through a lot these past few days, Corb, more than I thought. Even though I don't remember my past, I still feel something; I feel sad for your dad. What was his name? I asked, pausing on the road.

Corbin looked back, noticing me stop. "His name was Joseph," he said quietly under his breath as he turned back around and continued to walk.

A tear rolled down my cheek from the pain I could feel from Corbin as he mentioned his father's name. Clearing my throat and wiping my eyes, I began walking again, picking up my pace to catch up with him.

'As I was saying, you are one of us now, or should I say a part of my 'crew',' I said as I moved my fingers, smiling at him.

"Oh, is that right, I am a crew member? How delightful," he said, smiling to himself.

'You see there 'crew member', 'delightful'. Jesus, Corb, why do you have to speak so ancient, can't you be more urban?' I said as we came close to the car.

"Urban?" he said with a baffled look, the kind of look an elderly person gives when you are trying to help them understand technology.

'Jesus Christ, I am sorry it had to be said,' I blurted out waving my hands in the air to prevent him from getting angry; as my eyes met his fierce gaze. 'We have got some serious work to do, old man,' I muttered as we both opened the car doors and stepped in and shut them behind us.

"Okay, Alexa," he said, emphasizing my name. "Where did you last see your bag? Is that urban enough for you?"

'No, actually, just basic English but better than your ancient, but yes, I last had it when I was with those creepy agents; it must still be in the car,' I replied.

"Well, to the creepy agents it is then," he said as he pointed his finger in the air before starting the car. He seemed excited as if we were going off on an exciting new adventure…

'Ah! there you are,' I said as I saw my bag lying in the passenger's seat.

The drive was quite stretched on the way there, and luckily, there was no Taken in sight. We spent most of the time sharing stories getting to know each other. Corbin told me about all the countries he traveled to and the type of training he did. At one point, it seemed like he was a natural fighter, but then I saw right through him, and I knew he was lying. I told him how Jenna and I met, the things we went through in the home and when we broke out. How we got to where we are now, how I have always felt the urge to protect her, but after a while, I could not bear to talk about her; not knowing if she was dead or alive was killing me. I tried to teach him on stories and films he never heard of, gave him a taste of my world. I also managed to practice some words with him. It took nearly half an hour to get him to say what's up without sounding like a total creep.

I didn't realize how far we had gone till the drive; I must have been out for a while when the Taken took me.

As I stepped out of the car, I turned around and saw Corbin's back to me.

'What are you staring at?' I asked.

"So this is where the car turned off when you screamed," he said as he stared off into the dark pathway leading to the forest.

'Yes,' I answered barely, even speaking as the previous events began flashing through my eyes.

I led the way into the forest, walking down the hill; holding on to each tree, I tried to keep my balance. Everywhere I looked, I could see everything playback to me, the agents changing, Jenna running, the scream…

I threw on my bag and slammed the passenger door behind me to shake off the thoughts I was having and walked over to Corbin.

'What are you staring at?' I asked.

"This was the agent that tried to hurt you and Miss Jenna?" he asked sternly, sounding like a protective father.

'Yes, who...'

Before I could even finish, Corbin's hand was already up silencing me. I walked away when he did it, as that was just downright rude.

"To the cowardly, unbelieving, abominable, murderers, the sexually immoral, the sorcerers and idolaters and all liars, their place will be in the lake that burns with fire and Sulphur. This is the second death, Revelations chapter 21 verse 8," he recited as he lit the lighter that miraculously appeared in his hand, 'wait, was that my lighter?' I thought out loud.

I don't know how Corbin ended up with it, but the way he held on to it was a firm grip. He was angry, I could tell by the way his hand was clenching on to it. Corbin slowly lent down to the ground, picking up a twig, he lit it and threw it on to the fake agent James, then repeated the same words as he walked over to agent Norman.

Corbin was silent as he watched both of the corpse's burn, I couldn't take much more of it, so I decided to walk to the car and get reacquainted with an old friend.

'Ah, how much I have missed you?' I whispered as I looked at the spliff in between my fingers.

"Oh, I see why we really came back here," Corbin said as he came creeping out of the woods, scaring me.

'Oh Corb, don't do that. You scared the bajeebies out of me,' I moaned, utterly ignoring what he said.

"Bajee… never mind, and my apologies. What, nothing to say, eh?" Corbin looked at me with one of his eyebrows raised.

'I, I,' I stuttered, trying to fan out the spliff behind me. 'I, I, mean I needed the book, there may be important clues,' I continued with my back facing him, trying to hide the evidence.

"Hmmm… If you may say, there is no use hiding it. By the way, I can smell it in the air; it smells musty, hmmm… ripe," he said while trying to peak over my shoulder. "Oh, yes. How were you able to ignite? I am sure I heard you back there say I obtained your lighter. This was accidental as I came upon it resting on the floor."

'Corb, come on man, we spent hours practicing, what was that?' I said irritated. 'Wait, you have the lighter still?' I asked, cutting him off before he could attempt to respond.

"Yes, what have you been using?" he asked.

'I don't know,' I said as I leaned on to the car, thinking back to that moment. Experiencing quick flashes of myself holding on to the spliff in one hand and the other empty.

'I didn't have one, but the thing was always lit,' I mumbled, correcting myself to respect Corb.

"Fascinating," Corbin muttered.

'What?' I asked.

"I'll share with you in a moment, I just can't seem to find…"

'No, tell me,' I said interrupting him.

"Alexa, has anyone told you how impatient you are… any who you were able to light your 'Thing,'" he said while using his fingers. "You used your power, it has been getting stronger by the day, well, the night to be accurate. I thought it was controlled by your emotions, but you were able to set afire without realizing just because you were thinking about it."

'Okay, so what are you saying?' I said, waiting for the punch.

"I am saying," he said as he continued to pat his body over. "Sorry, I am saying that you weren't upset and you used your power, meaning it is not going to be difficult as I thought it would be to help you control it," he continued.

'Okay,' I said, still not getting where this conversation was going.

"God dammit!" Corbin blurted out "Oh, my apologies, Alexa, for cursing; forgive me."

'Wait, were you just attempting to be urban?' I chuckled.

"Yes, I am frustrated because I have somehow misplaced the keys, and yes, I have locked the doors," he said as he pulled the door handle.

'Oh, I see. Well, I have an idea,' I said excitedly like an eager cat, you know the kind in those cat and mouse chase cartoons and the cat has a great devious plan, and a light bulb appears above its head to show it is thinking. So much work going on in that head, so much electricity. Well, that was exactly how I was feeling.

'I realize now what you were trying to say and I agree I want to control it, so why not let me practice with the car?' I said, smiling with my eyes beaming at him.

"Very well," he said as he backed away from the car, keeping his eyes on me.

'What do I do?' I asked eagerly but confused.

"You need to empty your mind."

'That's easier said than done, especially with a mind like mine,' I interrupted then giggled.

Corbin's face was nothing but serious.

'Sorry,' I mumbled.

"You need to empty your mind and focus on the car," he continued.

I nodded and took a deep breath, closed my eyes, then opened them and exhaled.

'Car open now,' I said out loud feeling so stupid, but nothing happened.

I looked at Corbin.

"Focus on the car, focus all your energy on it, be the car."

'Really? Be the car?' I said with a smug look.

"I honestly don't know what I'm doing. I just saw this in a film once," Corb blurted out, trying to keep a straight face.

Just great. I'm supposed to be destined to be this Savior of the world with all these powers, and I don't have a clue on what I'm doing and my guide/protector/trainer/priest with complications doesn't know either. No, wait, he watched a film, so he's taking tips from it…

'I thought I was all-knowing, so why don't I know how to use my powers?' I asked, sounding confused with my confusion.

"Listen, Alexa," Corbin said while holding his head in his hand.

'Yes,' I said, my eyes locked on him, waiting for something meaningful to help.

"I didn't write the book, man," he said, sounding a bit too urban. "But I believe once you believe, everything will then fall into place, now focus.

I nodded not completely satisfied with his answer, I either created a monster or this man really was lying about being a priest because he didn't sound like Corbin just now; however, he was right!

I needed to believe in myself, I needed to focus, so I walked closer to the car with my hand resting against the door.

'NOW, OPEN!' I shouted, and before my eyes, the car flew back and up into the air then exploded, throwing both of us into the woods.

The sound of car burning was all I could hear as I laid there or the ground.

'Corb,' I cried out.

"Alexa? Maybe that was a little too much focus on the car, ey?" he called out.

'Yea,' I said, trying to laugh to show I was okay. 'Are you hurt?' I called out, worried about his answer.

"No," his voice called out closer than I expected and before I knew it, he was standing over me.

"Are you okay, Alexa?" he said as he rushed to help me to my feet.

'Yes, I think so; err, I mean yea, I was just checking out the stars,' I said as I walked passed him back to the road dusting off myself.

'What now?' I said as I stood there staring on to what used to be the car.

"We walk," Corbin said as he walked past me into the road.

I shrugged my shoulders and followed him.

'I'm sorry about your car,' I mumbled behind as we began our new journey…

CHAPTER NINE

PRACTICE, PRACTICE, AND YOU SHALL SUCCEED!

DARKNESS WITH A chill in the air, the sound of bones clicking is all I can hear, where is it coming from? The only sight of light I can see is flickering from a small box at the top of wherever I am. As my eyes follow the path, the flicker disappears just as my vision has adjusted, enabling me to make out this environment.

Filthy walls made up of old bricks, covered in moss and debris was all I could see at first, I realized after I was standing inside a room of some sort, a tiny one. Why am I here? What is that sound? Where is it coming from? Oh, welcome back my sequence of three, how I have missed you.

I walked towards the sounds I could hear, and as I got closer, the light reappeared flickering passed me, revealing a bed in front with a mysterious figure twitching as they lay.

I say twitching, but it wasn't quite; I couldn't tell at first, their back was facing me still laying down.

'Excuse me,' I called out pausing just before crashing into the bed.

The mysterious figure continued to cry as if I never spoke.

'Excuse me, are you okay?' I called out again speaking a little louder, but no response, just the same cry.

This was beginning to frustrate me; I get it they're upset and probably gone through something terrible, but to ignore me twice was just plain rude. I understand that I am the 'Savior' and all, but I don't have the patience for this kind of crap.

So, yeah, I tried to ignore my frustration and moved closer to the bed,

'Excuse me, are you okay? What happened? Why are you crying?' I said in my sequence of three, which was strange. I was sure I had overcome that disorder of my subconscious.

The mysterious figure ignored me again and continued to cry with a staggered hiss as they began shivering.

'LOOK,' I said in a loud, irritated tone. Taking a deep breath as my hand pressed hard against my face, 'I mean look,' I said again more calmly.

'If you just tell me what is wrong, maybe I can help you.'

The figure suddenly went silent, this annoyed the hell out of me, but I knew I had to be patient. I leaned closer trying to see their face, but their hair was blocking, and their back was still facing towards me.

'I know you don't know me, but I am here to help. It will be okay, I promise,' I said, feeling the urge to help and protect this person.

This all felt so familiar to me, this feeling I had, I sat there thinking why? Then it hit me 'Duh, Alexa, you're the Savior, it must be my power kicking in,' I said out loud to myself.

But was it? Was it really my powers? Had I really accepted who I was and the responsibility that came with it? I hoped so but sitting next to this stranger, saying those words made me feel comfortable like I was at home.

'Please, let me help you,' I whispered so naturally, not realizing, distracted by my thoughts. I sat there silently for a moment; I could feel something in me rising,

'Hey,' I said out loud snapping out of my daze as I grabbed their shoulder forcing them to look at me, and instantly, my heart was racing with so much speed I thought it was going to explode out of my chest, as the mysterious figures face was revealed.

"Alexa!" I heard a voice call out.

"Alexa!" it went again.

"Alexa, wake up, it is just a dream."

The voice became louder, it seemed familiar, opening my eyes slowly. I saw Corbin leaning over me with both of his hands on each end of my shoulders.

'Corb,' I struggled to say, 'why?' I thought, realizing after how dehydrated I was, and my upper body felt questionably ruffled. Before I could process what could have happened, I started to feel my body being shaken.

"Alexa, wake up!!" he shouted.

'I am up,' I thought.

My eyes were open; couldn't he see me? I could see him, so clear as day. I was looking right at him in his eyes, but it was as if I wasn't there.

'STOP!' I shouted.

"Alexa!" Corbin replied.

Suddenly my eyes opened again, but I had no memory of closing them, how strange? Yeah, I know.

'Corbin, what happened?' I asked, confused.

"You had a bad dream, do you remember?" he replied.

'Bad dream...oh yes,' I said realizing I had been distracted by what just happened; that I had forgotten about the mysterious figure.

'It was a dream,' I whispered. 'I, I remember I saw this, wait,' I paused realizing how horrible I felt. I was hot dripping in a puddle of sweat; I didn't even notice how out of breath I was.

I looked on the bed, then around the room we were hiding in, books were lying everywhere, chairs were knocked to the ground, a mirror and picture frames that were previously on the wall were now on the floor, broken.

I took a deep breath and exhaled slowly 'What happened in here, Corb?' I croaked out my mouth dry.

"I was in the lavatory freshening up, and I heard sounds of shatters and cracks, I feared for your safety, so I came charging in, and I began to see furniture flying across the room, some were just floating. I have never in my life seen something so remarkable, I was so amazed that I nearly forgot about you and where you resided.

Then there you were, laying there, beads of sweat dripping down your face, hands balled up into fists gripping onto your quilt and your head twitching left to right uncontrollably. At once, it came to my attention that you were the reason for everything going on in this room, Miss Alexa. Sorry I'm, I'm still in shock," he explained.

"What was your dream? It wasn't the same one, was it?" he asked, concerned.

'Yes, it was,' I replied. 'But it seemed so real this time; I felt it, I touched the person... I felt...' I said drifting off in my sentence.

"What is it?" Corbin said in an anxious, concerned tone.

'I, err, when I was dreaming I heard you, I heard you calling me, and I opened my eyes, I told you I was awake, but you ignored me,' I said trying to make sense with what I was trying to say. 'Why would you continue to shake me like that, like I am a doll with no feelings. Just because I'm the Savior doesn't mean I am indestructible. Well, obviously, I am, but I have feelings, and I do feel pain Cathy,' I said feeling angrier as I spoke.

"My apologies, Alexa, for hurting you, but I do not know of what you speak; your eyes were always closed until this moment that you woke, you never spoke either, you were just uncontrollably twitching, showing no response to my calls; I had been calling you for nearly five minutes," he explained.

'I, I don't understand,' I said, I had a feeling on what it was, but I just didn't feel like saying it out loud, not exactly yet.

"I will help you find clarity, Alexa, but the previous events have caused a disturbance. Many would have heard, and they will be coming soon; we should move to a different location," he said as he hopped off the bed and started gathering his things.

'Does that mean I can't have a shower?' I said in a whiney tone.

"I'm afraid so, Alexa."

'But I am completely soaking in sweat, Corb.'

"Sorry, I promise once we find a new location, we will get you some new clothes and a bath."

'Fine,' I said as I crawled out of bed grabbing my boots and my jacket. 'Could you at least pass me the bottle of water, I feel so dehydrated,' I said as I slid on my boots; I felt disgusting and exhausted.

The last few, well, to be honest, I didn't know what it was, if it had been hours or days or weeks, I couldn't tell you. Since this whole shit started, it had been dark ever since, they weren't kidding when they prophesied about the darkness coming, I never realized they meant it literally, it was as if the sun had died and time had stopped.

So yes, the last few timeless nights were a continuous disaster. I was supposed to be practicing how to control my power, but it was so hard to concentrate with so many obstacles in our way.

From being on the run from the Taken, having to travel most of our journey on foot or the recurring thought of not knowing if Jenna was dead or alive eating away at me. After I blew up the first car, yes the first, there was many more after that, but I'll explain later. So, after the first car being blown to smithereens, Corbin and me, was forced to continue our journey on foot. A period in our journey that felt like we had been walking for centuries; but we still found a way to make use of it. Corbin tried to teach me how to balance my emotions, he told me there's no right way for him to teach me on how to control my powers, as in reality who is he to teach when he does not have the power. Which he was right, I couldn't disagree, but at the same time, it frustrated me as it seemed like we had been spending too many timeless nights together and my weakened spirit had rubbed off on him a little too much for my liking.

He believed once I can balance my emotions and honestly believe in myself, then everything would fall into place. If I was given a bag of weed for every time, he said that I would have an unlimited supply by now. He was becoming like one of those annoying songs that you grow to like at first then by the 4th or 5th time, you can't take the sound of it anymore. Yes, that was Corbin.

"Believe in yourself."

"Self-preservation is the key."

"Be the energy."

"Use the force."

That was Corbin over and over, for someone that claimed to not know a lot about modern entertainment, he used many quotes from many movies I had seen. When I brought it up, he would talk himself out of it and end up telling me more stories about the bible and the trials and tribulations he had to go through over the years.

I remember when I was 17, it was a few months after Jenna and I had escaped the system, we had shacked up in an old building in the city far away from 'the home', we had nothing but the clothes on our backs and a few snacks we had stolen from the cafeteria.

When Jenna would go to sleep, I'd go out on to the rooftop outside and watch all the people like, families coming back from family stuff that families do. There were these two particular people I'd see every Tuesday night at 9 o'clock sharp, a man and a young girl; she looked about my age or a little younger. She'd be walking with him side by side, hand in hand. They would always be laughing, he would say something to her, and her eyes would light up as he smiled at her and she at him. I always dreamed about what their conversations could have been about, what a father could be saying to his daughter, I envied them, I wanted and wished to have a life just like that; a bond.

Over time I grew angry with life, with my mother and father for abandoning me and with myself for wishing for something that could never happen. As I walked by Corbin's side, I thought of the father and daughter, I then thought of Corbin and I, for a single moment, it felt nice. But be careful what you wish for and do not wish for another person's life just because of the way the picture looks. Don't judge a book by its cover. Believe me, I had to learn the hard way as I later came to realize that the father and daughter I mentioned were actually a man and a young prostitute that had come to a weekly arrangement… disgusting, I know. I didn't know till one Tuesday night when I saw them down an alleyway. It took me a while to understand what was actually going on, but eventually, I realized.

So yes, during our timeless journey back to Corbin's 'Secret Corner,' we faced many obstacles, due to the lack of transport; we spent some time walking in the darkness. You'd think someone who's had time to get used to this upcoming apocalypse would be okay with the dark, but unfortunately, that wasn't the case; it was shocking, no disturbing to watch Corbin be afraid of the dark. That's right, the priest/hitman/ ninja/protector was fearful of the dark, how he kept it a secret this whole time still baffles me.

After learning his secret, after taunting him about it, after crying from laughter, I later found myself determined to find a car to have a source of light to calm his nerves, but the problem was, we were so far from the town that there wasn't a car in sight. I even, at one point, offered him a spliff to help calm his nerves. Yeah, a foolish mistake I know; what kind of dumbass offers a priest drugs? And even though his faith was complicated, that could have been the dumbest idea I have ever had in my life; I actually thought he was going to kill me in that instant for even suggesting it.

I even tried to make myself set alight or as Corbin calls it all 'glowy', I hated that term, he was the man, and I was the girl, yet his name was so girly; no wonder why his parents named him Cathy. But yes, I tried to go all 'glowy' but nothing happened. I tried my hardest to focus, to control my power, I pushed and pushed and the only thing I managed to do was make the biggest embarrassing sound from my butt. Yeah, I farted, I made myself fart....

After a few miles of suffering from the sound of the increased speed of Corbin's heart rate, we came across a car. So determined to help Corbin with his fear and eager to see progression within my power, I walked over to the car to give it another try.

"Miss... Alexa," Corbin said while clearing his throat.

"Maybe I should try this time."

'What? I was only going to see if it is unlocked,' I said in an irritated tone as I placed my hand on the bonnet, and suddenly the car began to melt.

"Jesus Christ," he shouted.

'Corb,' I shouted in an angry tone.

"Why did you have to go do that?" he whined. "I felt so relieved to see it and now..." he cut off mid-sentence placing his head into his hands.

'So what, I can't even touch things now,' I said in a frustrated tone as I stared at my hands.

"Alexa, please can you remain calm," Corbin said, creating a distance between us.

At first, I felt offended and hurt thinking he was afraid of me. I realized after the lamp posts, the buildings ahead, the signs hanging and the trees were all shaking.

'Oh sorry,' I said as I inhaled and exhaled slowly and gradually, everything around us went calm.

"Hey, good job, that inhaling stuff seems to work, we can use that when we practice, and sorry about before, I didn't realize there are two cars ahead... But just hang back, I will see if I can get it started," he said as he bolted off leaving me behind.

So, he got the car started woohoo... a few... Let's just say 'hours' later, we arrived at a familiar looking area, then all of sudden Corbin stopped the car abruptly.

'What, why...

"Please, don't go back to that, you've been doing so well," Corbin interrupted.

'What. I wasn't going to. Oh, whatever! Why did you stop?' I replied.

"Something doesn't feel right, I can sense it," he whispered as he stepped out the car.

I watched him with the straightest face through the passenger window, thinking of why he is whispering. I hesitated, rolled my eyes and followed after him.

'What do you mean?' I whispered as I caught up behind him.

'Corb!'

Corbin froze as he got closer to the tunnel leading to the secret corner.

'Corb, what do you sense?'

"I'm, trying to… err, I'm trying to remember if I locked the door."

'What?' I said in a confused tone.

"I said I am trying to remember if I locked the door," he whispered as he began strolling into the tunnel.

'Corb, why are we whispering, why would you need to lock it?' I said as I watched him walk ahead of me.

"Ssshhh… Wait here, I'll be right back," he said as he disappeared into the darkness.

'Wait, shouldn't I go? I am the Savior after all,' I called out but it was too late; he was gone. I could hear his heart beat so fast, the sound of the heart rate increasing as he moved further away and then nothing.

'Corb!'

'Corb!'

'Shit!'

I was beginning to lose it. Why in the hell did I let him walk away? Why didn't I just go after him? Why am I still standing here asking myself these questions? Because I was terrified, but even more scared knowing his secret but I remained frozen.

A few minutes had passed, nothing but the sound of my breathing then without a warning, panting, deep breaths getting more profound, the sound of feet smacking the floor getting louder and louder.

"Alexa, run!" Corbin shouted out as he appeared out from the darkness, with dozens of the Taken following behind him.

I ran as fast as I could, trying to get to the car. I am starting to get tired of these random moments I have of speed, as the normal me is not that great at running. My heart pounded aggressively as I leapt over the car to the driver's door, I touched the handle...

'Shit... Why now? Why?' I cried out as I realized I somehow locked all the doors of the car and the keys were still in the ignition.

'Come on, please open.'

'Open sesame.'

'Abracadabra'

"Alexa, why are you not starting the car?" Corbin shouted as he got closer.

'I, I accidentally locked the car,' I replied nervously. 'Just give me a moment.'

'Car, open now!' I shouted.

"No," Corbin called out, but it was too late as we both watched the car lift up off the ground and fly into the direction of Corbin and the Taken.

'Corb,' I screamed as I watched the car go towards them, my eyes closed then opened.

'Where am I?' I whispered to myself. It's dark ahead of me; there's nothing but darkness and behind me in the other direction is a light coming from the headlights of the car.

'It wasn't real,' I whispered. 'It wasn't real. Shit!' I continued to get excited knowing my power has increased, then I heard it, the sound of panting, the sound of dozens of feet smacking against the floor.

'It's happening,' I whispered. 'Why am I still talking to myself? I need to run now.'

So I begin running towards the car, this time making sure I don't jump over it and I am calm.

"Alexa, run!" I can hear Corbin shouting in the background.

'I am way ahead of you, Corb,' I shouted out as I got closer to the car.

'Now inhale and exhale,' I say to myself trying to remain calm, my hand trembling.

I touched the handle slowly and calmly, then 'click' is all I hear, the sound of each lock around the car locking itself.

'I CAN'T BELIEVE THIS SHIT AAHHH!' I screamed out in frustration.

'I saw this, I saw it. Why couldn't I change it? Why?' I moaned as I bashed my fits against the car which was an idiotic move as that lead the car to break down, and when I say break down, I mean all the tires popped, the windows smashed and the bonnet set alight.

'No, no, no.'

"Alexa, what are you doing?" I could hear Corb screeching at me, but I was too angry to take notice of him; I was blood angry. It was as if I had become the hulk and I wanted to smash. I could feel something come over me. As I looked towards Corbs' direction, I looked at him then through him. Everything looked different; I could see the fine detail in the atmosphere, the particles floating around us, the tiny fragments of life that can't be seen by the naked eye. I looked at the Taken chasing Corbin, I could see into their souls, I could see their true nature, their secrets, their sins, it made me sick, it made me angry.

I looked at Corbin again, closed my eyes, then opened them, I looked at the car placing my hand and shouted 'CAR OPEN NOW!'

I watched as the car lifted upward flying into the direction of the Taken, I watched as the car exploded just as it hit the unwanted crowd blowing them into pieces, I remember looking up at the sky; no stars, no light. Why was I looking up? Oh, yes, the impact of the blow knocked me to the ground. Am I dead?

'Ow, my head,' I moaned as I sat up off the ground.

I looked ahead of me, the sound of the car alarm echoing in my ears, which was amazing to me how I still seemed to work after the collision. All I could see were bodies lying scattered all over the ground, some pieces of the car lodged into their bodies and faces, it was disgusting to look at, and I could sense I was feeling sorry for them. A few just lying pathetically and dying slowly, then it hit me; where was Corbin?

'Corb?' I shouted as I stepped to my feet.

'Corbin!' I shouted again with so much panic in my voice.

'Oh, my god, where is he? Did I kill him? Did his body disintegrate from the explosion? How could that be possible when the Taken were left burning on the ground?'

I stood there frozen pondering on what could have happened, and then suddenly, I could feel myself vibrating.

'What is that?' I said, all freaked out with what it could be.

I began patting myself when I realized I wasn't vibrating, but my pocket was; it was my phone ringing.

'Wow, you're actually working,' I said as I took out the phone which was a mystery as I could have sworn it died after Jenna was taken, then again if I am honest, I forgot I even had it. It surprises me that it is still in one piece considering all I have been through since the night it all started. It seems like such a long time ago now, that was the past and now this is my present, my future; this permanent hell. No, hell has light. All that fire, so they claim. Yeah, I know what you're thinking. How do I know that, right? I do read; Well, I did in the home, considering the kind it was. I often read the Bible, and I read about hell, but this wasn't hell; this dark, black, cold, lonely place, it was nothingness!

So, I stared at my phone, forgetting to do the most obvious action, which was actually answering it. Snapping out of my daze, I touched the screen to respond, eager on whom could be trying to call me, in that instant the screen cracked.

'No,' I screamed. 'Please fix, please,' I moaned nervously as I held the phone in my shaking hand.

All that caused the phone to crush into a ball in my hands as if there was an invisible person in front of me bullying me.

'Arrrrgggh!' I screamed out while tossing the phone into the air.

'Can't you do anything right?'

'Corbin,' I cried as I dropped to my knees, I was so frustrated and tired. I stared at the ground and punched it with my fists, each hit left a print of my fist behind, the ground started to crack, and the holes got deeper.

My eyes filled with tears, I couldn't take it anymore Corbin was dead, Jenna was killed, I was supposed to defeat this evil, and I wasn't even ready. I continued to cry and beat the ground, not realizing the rain that had started and the thunder attacking the sky, and then I heard him.

"Alexa," he called out.

'God, is that you?' I screamed out. 'Why aren't you helping? Why?'

"Alexa"

"Corb?" I called out as I sat there on the ground in the rain.

"Alexa!" I could hear his voice getting closer. I looked up into the direction of the tunnel, the flames from the car and dead bodies were dying down due to the rain making it hard to make out who was coming.

"Alexa, are you okay?" the voice said again as he got closer. It was Corb, it had to be, it sounded like him.

'Corb, is that you? Please, stay away; it's not safe, I'm not safe,' I said as my eyes dropped back to the ground.

"Nonsense, I will never turn my back on you," he replied as he got close, then I looked up, and it was him, it was Corbin.

'No,' I screamed, my power and anger knocked him to the ground.

'Corbin, I'm so sorry, but please stay away, please. There is something wrong with me, I can't control it, I tried, I really have.' But everything I do goes wrong. I'm not cut out for this, I'm not ready for all of this, I thought I killed you Corb, I nearly killed you just now,' I cried out, more tears falling down my face.

"Miss Alexa, just calm down."

'I am calm!' I shouted, and with that, more thunder broke through the clouds.

"Ssshhh… Just breathe, this not your fault and your powers are only imbalanced due to you, your emotions, your state of mind. When was the last time you even slept? Ate? That is the cause for all of this," he explained.

'Really? I said, trying to hold back my tears.

"Yes, think about it; when your body hasn't recharged or had food to replace the energy and sugar you've lost, what do you do? You find it difficult to concentrate on tasks you normally perform, mistakes are made, and this is the reason for your suffering. And you didn't kill me, you beamed me into the Secret corner; when I say beam, I mean projected... err teleport, yes, teleported."

'I know what you mean Corbin,' I screamed causing the street lamps to smash.

"Hey, breathe Alexa, yes, you are not fully ready but look how far you come, look how much you have accomplished, someone who only found out just a few nights ago and now look at you, you've saved me from the Taken, you saved us just now," he said as he took a few steps closer.

'Step back, Corbin please, what if I melt you? I didn't want to be this fucking Savior. I didn't ask for this, it's not fair, I don't want this, I just want to go back to my old life, it wasn't much, but it was still mine, and I had control over it. Why am I doing God's job?' I said as my eye returned to the ground.

"Look, even though it is complicated for me right now, I can't speak for him, but he always has a plan," he replied.

'You can't even justify why God has sent me to do a job he can easily do with the click of his fingers,' I screamed back at him.

Corbin remained silent while I continued to sob.

'I even burnt all of the things,' I mumbled.

"Alexa, you didn't, I have them with me, you sent them to the secret corner with me. Don't you see how in control you really are? You are the Savior, you just need to rest, and look, there must be something to help calm you? Hmm… where is your grass?" he said as he set my bag down in front of me.

'Grass?' I asked in a confused tone.

"Yes, grass, the thing that you ingest?" he replied confidently.

'What?'

"The thing that you smoke, Alexa," he said in a stern tone, and with that, I burst into laughter, and the rain and thunder around us suddenly disappeared.

'Corb, it is called weed,' I said, continuing to laugh.

"Grass, weed; what's the difference between them? I can't believe I am encouraging it, but maybe if you smoke it, you will be able to relax, and you can take a nap in the car," he said as he pushed the bag closer to me.

Afraid of what may happen, I dragged myself against the ground backing away from Corbin and the bag 'I can't, Corbin, I just can't touch anything, I'm not safe.'

"Then what do you suggest? You need to get stoned," he said while scratching his head. "I can't believe I just said that, I am so going to hell".

'Maybe its best we should part ways, I'm no good to anyone,' I said feeling defeated and pathetic, the rain returned around me.

"NONSENSE! YOU ARE ALEXANDRA NEMESIA, YOU ARE THE CHOSEN ONE, AND I AM YOUR GUIDE AND PROTECTOR," he shouted.

"I am sorry, but you need to stop feeling sorry for yourself and suck it up. I'll prepare your weeds if you are afraid to touch it, but if you think for an instant that I'd leave you behind, you are wrong. Just wait here, DO NOT GO ANYWHERE," Corbin continued.

'Okay, okay, I won't go anywhere; just stop shouting at me,' I moaned, afraid to wipe my eyes, afraid what my hands would do.

A few minutes had passed from when Corbin left me after his huge lecture. I felt like a spoilt child that had just been told off from her dad for the very first time, I felt sad and insecure but afraid to get upset again just in case he caught me and shouts at me again. I didn't like this side of Corbin; so stern, no patience. A few minutes later, I could hear the sound of an engine but from where? That was the question. I wanted to stand up and investigate, but I felt so drained, so useless. What was the point? I'd probably ruin whatever I decided to do, so I waited, I looked towards the tunnel but nothing, where was Corbin?

Shortly after a car came from around the corner, my heart began to race; what if it was another pair of dodgy Taken 'agents'? I wanted to move, I tried to speak, but I was frozen. I could hear the sound of the door open, the sound of a foot reach out and touch the ground, the door wasn't closed behind, my eyes on the ground, and my heart racing as the footsteps grew closer.

"My apologies on the wait, I was having trouble locating the keys," the voice said. I looked up, and it was Corbin. "My god, Alexa, why do you look like you have just seen a ghost"?

'I, I thought you were the Taken. I couldn't move, I couldn't do anything,' I said crying into my lap.

"My apologies I should have said I was going to get the car. I have been preparing for this day, and I had a backup car parked in a garage around the corner," he said as he knelt down into my bag.

'I don't understand; why do we need a car, where are we going?' I asked as I watched him.

"We can't stay here, Alexa, not anymore, because it's not safe. Those things found it and the noise of the explosion would have alerted many; we must find somewhere safe so you can rest. I've been so busy trying to prepare you but I haven't paid enough attention to your needs, you are still human after all, well, sort of. I am sorry I haven't been doing a good job as your protector, so how do we do this now?" he said as he pulled out my weed box staring at in confusion.

'Corb, don't be silly, you've been doing great considering the circumstances,' I said as I pointed at the items he needed to use to make my spliff. I honestly felt embarrassed and terrible, having a priest make a spliff for me, it is something I never saw myself doing or even imagined. This was the most awkward moment I think I could ever have with Corbin; I will always appreciate him for it.

"Okay, there we go; not bad for an amateur, ay?" He said, smiling proudly of his work. "Okay, please tell me you have something to ignite, I thought I had the other one, I don't remember giving it back. I would ask for you to try and light it like you did that time, but I don't think that will be a good idea," he said as he held onto the spliff as if it was a pair of dirty knickers.

"Wait, it's okay I've got it here," he said, waving the lighter in the air.

Corbin walked over to me and placed the spliff in my mouth; he then lit it for me then removed it when I was ready to exhale.

"How do you feel now?" He asked eagerly.

'Really, Corb, you just lit it, it doesn't work that quickly,' I said in an annoyed tone, and before I knew it, the rain around me stopped. I began to feel more drained than before. No, I am wrong, not drained but relaxed, at ease; for an amateur Corbin made some intense shit.

"Don't underestimate me, Miss Alexa, I can see the stone has taken over you," he said while smiling.

A few minutes had passed, Corbin continued to help me smoke, I was too afraid to touch anything, still convinced I'd make it melt. Suddenly, Corbin left the spliff in my mouth and began cradling me in his arms.

Shocked but unable to talk with the spliff in my mouth, I had to take the risk and used one of my hands to remove it, 'What the hell are you doing?' I said.

“She speaks,” he says as he lifted me up off the ground. “I’m sorry, Alexa, but we need to move.”

‘But you just touched me.’

“I took the risk, and I’m fine, you touched the spliff and you’re fine, enough arguing. When I put you in the car, you will have a nap, I’ve already laid a pillow and blanket in the back,” he said sounding more like a demand.

‘Fine.’

So, yes, that's how we ended up in that room, well, motel if to be precise; the Imperial 400 motel located in Newburgh, New York. It wasn't that fancy, then again, I don't remember much as I was asleep most of the journey. And when we arrived, I must have been sleepwalking. From what Corbin shared with me, apparently I was up and told him about my dream and even asked for hot dogs, but I don't remember those details, so yes, I'll justify it as sleepwalking.

So, here we were on the run again to find a place to recharge and gather supplies, I was beginning to feel like the people from one of those zombie apocalypse shows, scrounging like tramps for scraps; I didn't understand why it's not like the world ended centuries ago and everything had either been taken or dried out. But no, Corbin wanted to be cautious, he didn't want to risk going into stores just in case the Taken could be waiting to ambush us. If I had my way, we would have a mini caravan with an abundant supply of food and weed stocked up in the rooms, and Jenna and I would be in the back relaxing as Corbin drives us to safety... Jenna…

"Alexa"

"Alexa"

'Yes,' I said, startled by Corbin shouting at me. 'Why are you shouting?' I asked.

"I have been calling you for a few minutes now," he said in an annoyed tone. "I'm starting to believe you have some sort of selective hearing, which I do not find amusing," he continued.

'Oh, sorry Corb, keep your knickers on,' I giggled. 'Why were you calling me?'

"I asked you a question, and I do not wear knickers, Mr. Alexa," he said with a cheeky grin.

'Oh, was that you trying to retaliate? Oh my, you got me soooo bad,' I said sarcastically.

'So what did you ask?'

"What happened in your dream? You said it felt so real this time," he asked while rolling his eyes, and yes, he was rolling them even though he was driving and his eyes were on the road, I could tell by the twitch on his cheek.

'Oh, well.... what have I shared with you? I don't remember our conversation,' I replied

"Well, let's see you were. Err, yes, it was…hmmm.. my apologies, Alexa, I have forgotten the details we shared," Corbin said.

'Oh, fine, I'll start from the beginning, but first, is there a reason why we are still driving? We have passed many buildings,' I said as I looked out the window.

"Oh, no reason, I just missed the drive," he said while clearing his throat.

'Really, Corbin, I smell and feel horrible; you promised me a bath,' I moaned.

"Ok, ok, just give me 10 minutes, tell me about your dream, and once you are done, we can stop," he said.

'Fine, that seems reasonable,' I said sarcastically. 'Where do I begin? Hmmm, well, I remember I am in this room, I can hear crying coming from somewhere, but I do not know where. Then there is a light flickering, so I follow it, as I walk closer I see a bed ahead of me, someone is lying there, their back is towards me, and they are shivering. I call out to them over and over, but they ignore me, I remember feeling frustrated because of it, but at the same time the urge to protect this stranger,' I explained.

"Hmmm, interesting! Is that it?" Corbin asked.

‘No, there’s more, I continue to speak to this stranger who remains silent but still shivers, I remember the urge to protect them; it felt so familiar to me as if I knew this person. Then I don’t know, I just got impatient and I snapped at them, then pulled their shoulder to look at me,’ I said as I stare off into the darkness.

“And?” Corbin mumbled.

‘And what?’ I said, baffled.

“And what did you see as you pulled the person towards you? Wake up Alexa,” Corbin snapped.

‘Oh, sorry! Easy Corb, you are becoming very moody, maybe you need a nap,’ I said.

“My apologies and maybe you’re right, I haven’t entirely been looking after myself, but yes, what did you see?”

‘Well, I…. that’s it, I saw nothing, there was no face, no nothing.’

“That’s it? That’s what caused you to trash the motel?” he said, snarkily.

‘Oh, I’m sorry, Corbin, have you seen someone with no face before?’ I said in a defensive tone.

“I’m sorry, Alexa, but it was just a dream, no need to be so dramatic,” he said as we pulled up into a side road, where are we now... That’s right, Liberty town, a town in Sullivan County, New York.

‘Whatever,’ I grunted. ‘So why here? Why this dump?’ I asked as I looked up at the building in front of me.

“Why do you assume there?” he asked.

‘I don’t know, I just… I feel it,’ I replied.

“Hmm, marvelous. The Savior is all-knowing,” he said excitedly.

‘So, I see you’re going back to that, can we just get inside, and this doesn’t look like a place that has a bathroom or clothes, Corb.’

"Let's just see once we get inside, look over there, the door is open," he said as he pointed into the direction.

I rolled my eyes and began to walk towards the building, just a few steps closer, and I would have been inside, then suddenly, Corbin dragged me back, putting his hand over my mouth.

'What are you doing?' I said, feeling startled.

"My apologies but something is not right, I have a feeling we are not alone," Corbin explained.

'Great, I don't understand, this is the second time you have 'sensed' something, how? When I am supposed to be the Savior, how are you sensing them and I'm not? Do you have powers? Is there something you're not telling me?' I blurted out.

"Whoa, calm down Alexa, and no, I do not have powers. How I sense things is a mystery to me, maybe it is due to me being a priest, and I don't know, years of experience maybe," Corbin said reassuringly.

'Okay, but it doesn't make sense, how can I sense you chose this place, but I can't sense the Taken?' I asked in a frustrated tone.

"Well, maybe it's because we know each other, we have a connection..." Corbin said as he watched the building.

'Corb, that doesn't even make sense, you know that right? I am the Savior; I should sense the Taken if I'm supposedly all-knowing.' I said as I walked back to the car.

"Alexa…I'm just making this up as I go, there wasn't no manual on how to train the 'Savior', or how your power manifests, cut me some slack," he snapped.

'Making it up as you go, really Corb… that's reassuring, and how can you say there is no manual? Isn't that what the black book is? A manual of my life.'

"Not exactly, but enough of this talk, and no, this is not me being moody, Alexa. We need to think of a plan."

'What kind of plan?' I asked.

"A plan to get them out, I know they are in there, I can feel it," said Corbin.

'Why? Can't we just go somewhere else?' I moaned.

"No, it has to be this one."

'But why?' I pressed.

"Because of the higher ground and erm… to be honest, I'm so tired I just want to get it over with, I can't be asked to go somewhere else," he said tiresomely.

'Okay, so what do you suggest?' I asked in an irritated tone. It was really getting to me how Corbin was taking the lead with this whole senses' thing, jealousy maybe, the case of the green eye they would say. I am grown enough to admit that I envied him a little, I'm supposed to be this Savior, and I'm struggling with control over my powers, and Corbin, on the other hand, was an ordinary being and he could sense when the Taken was near… it didn't make sense and believe me, it was frustrating, but I trust him and appreciate him for everything he's done.

"Alexa!" Corbin shouted.

'Yes,' I replied.

"Did you get that?"

'Get what,' I asked, confused.

"Jesus, Alexa, you need to stop allowing yourself to get distracted and focus," Corbin complained, I rolled my eyes and looked at him ready to listen. "Right, here is the plan….

CHAPTER TEN

HERE COMES THE SAVIOR!

OH MY GOD, oh my god, breathe, Alexa, breathe, inhale, exhale, inhale, exhale. Oh, it's not working, all I want to do is scream, but I can't because if I do, they will all hear me, then more will come, and I'm not ready for that yet.

'Come on, Alexa,' I whisper. 'Just follow the plan, don't screw this up,' I continued with my back to the wall. I was hiding from the Taken, the plan was to get their attention and lure them out… that's right; Corbin's genius plan was for me to be the bait. That's right, me the 'SAVIOR' had to be the bait, the damsel in distress, while Corbin played the knight in shining armor.

I was skeptical about the whole idea when I first walked in; I couldn't even see a thing. I remember the smell; it was some sort of metallic scent. I could hear the sound of clicking echoing throughout the building, the sounds of the Taken breathing and moaning. And the sound of my heart beating so fast and loudly travelled in between the echoes, I'm surprised they couldn't hear the beats of my heart or that I didn't die from it ripping out my chest at the rate it was going.

I continued to walk down the hallway; Corbin's genius plan was for me to stumble upon the Taken like a frightened little girl and make them chase me out of the building where he would do the rest.

'Smart,' right? I know. Firstly, how could I stumble upon them when it was pitch-black, and I couldn't see a thing? And I'm not even a little girl; I am over 6foot.

Secondly, how was I supposed to lead them out when there was more than one floor in this building unless I'm expected to lure them out floor after floor? He wasn't too clear on the details of that part unless he was… I do remember zoning out at one point when he was speaking, if he did say something important it's pointless now, I am already inside and whatever he instructed is a mystery to me.

I stopped walking as I came to a hallway with two directions 'This is annoying,' I whispered.

There must be something, I thought, and then it hit me, why don't I try to go all glowy? I'd defiantly be able to navigate in this creepy building. I tried and tried but nothing, not even an embarrassing fart this time. 'Just great,' I muttered before taking a right down the hallway. I began walking again, moaning to myself as I stroked the walls to navigate; I was so irritated and tired of it all, I couldn't understand why I was struggling to control my powers, I had accepted who I really was, I was even training, after all, so why the constant errors? Why? Why? Why?

Why all these questions that I can't even answer myself when I was supposedly all-knowing? How could I be all-knowing when I had no clue what I was doing? When would I be all-knowing? It just didn't make any sense. How could Corbin sense evil and I couldn't?

I couldn't even sense when my battery was low on my phone till it was too late and ended up dying on me when I needed it the most. I couldn't sense a damn thing; well, I could sense his emotions, but that is only because I'm just good with people and their body language… Wait, I thought, something didn't feel right, the smell of metallic had intensified, and my chest felt tight like I had trapped wind. No, not exactly that, but it felt like heartburn, but not exactly that either, it can't be explained, it was bizarre.

Then it hit me, the sound of breathing around me. I started to concentrate on wanting to see in the dark, suddenly my eyes had changed, and I could see. Which was a mistake when I saw the Taken ahead of me, but that wasn't the most frightening thing as I realized the heavy breathing wasn't coming from the ones ahead but above me. I tilted my head up to the ceiling and saw dozens of the Taken staring at me.

One after the other, the Taken fell from the ceiling landing onto their feet in front of me while some remained, others started to crawl down the walls beside me. Is it possible to be consumed with so much fear that it can kill you? Because that was how I felt at that moment, afraid and dead. My body was still, no breaths, no sweat, zilch, it was as if I had been struck by Medusa and turned to stone and no, not an exaggeration. I was screaming at myself to move, to do something but I just couldn't.

'Thump' went the sound of another Taken dropping from the ceiling landing right in front of me. It looked right in my face into my eyes, I still remained motionless with my heart aching. It moved closer, its body clicking and snapping out of place, its mouth opened I assume; it was about to make a loud roar or to order the others to devour me, I don't know, I don't speak Taken…

But yes, as soon as it attempted to speak, 'bam' was all I heard. Its mouth began dripping with blood, and a hole was in between its eyes, then suddenly the rest became chaotic, moaning and shuffling throughout the hallway.

"Alexa!" I heard a voice shout, but I remained still.

"Alexa, run now!" the voice shouted again, it was Corbin. Somehow hearing his voice brought my body back to reality, everything I should have been feeling came crashing in me, the sweat, the excessive heart rate, the hyperventilating.

I took a step back slowly, and in sync, the Taken moved too.

"Move now," Corbin shouted, which was annoying because I was trying to, something he obviously couldn't see.

I took a few more steps back, and the Taken followed, the sound of scratching on the walls as they shuffled flooded through my ears.

"For the love of Christ," I heard Corbin mutter then the sound of a gunshot followed behind me, a little too close for my liking. I peeped my head over my shoulder and right behind me was one of the Taken.

"Alexa!"

I could hear the desperation and fear he had for my life in his voice.

I took a deep breath as I turned around to the thing behind me, I lifted up my leg and kneed it right in its private parts if it even still exists and I ran past towards Corbin.

"WHAT WAS THAT?" Corbin shouted as I got closer to him, ignoring all the Taken that was following behind. "IT WAS DEAD, AND WHAT IN JESUS NAME WERE YOU DOING OVER THERE? I GAVE YOU ONE JOB HONESTLY!" he continued as he fired at the Taken who was getting a little too close.

I was right before, Corbin needed a nap, he was getting unbearable to be around, and I couldn't take it anymore, the continuous shouting at me like I was a child.

'DO NOT SPEAK OF THY LORD'S NAME IN VAIN!!!' I shouted, knocking Corbin and the Taken behind me to the floor.

Whoa…. I know, I said that I don't even know what came over me, I didn't usually care about that sort of stuff, but I was just so angry. Corbin looked at me in shock, I could sense so many things from him, one was excitement then I realized I had gone all glowy.

'I see,' I muttered silently acknowledging the glow around me, I could hear the Taken getting to their feet.

'Corbin, leave now,' I instructed.

"What, why?" he asked, confused.

'Leave NOW!' I shouted startling him; I could feel the 'glow' expanding within me. 'I'm sorry but just go hide, please I don't think I can hold it in any longer'.

I know the term hold it in any longer sounds like I am holding in a big fart or something, but it wasn't that, obviously. I just felt like I was a computer and I had been set to self-destruct, implode. Corbin nodded and got to his feet then made a run for it, I could hear his breaths, his heartbeat then he was gone. I turned around and watched on to the Taken who was charging towards me, an angry mob. I closed my eyes and let out a deep breath…

Hmmmm, where am I? Darkness with a sinister chill in the air, and the sound of bones clicking is all I hear...

Filthy walls made up of old bricks, covered in moss and debris was all I could see at first. I realized after I was standing inside a room of some sort, a tiny one. Why am I here? What is that sound? Where is it coming from? Oh, great, I guess I am dreaming again. Why do I keep having this same dream? Oh, well, might as well let it play out to see what it means. I look around, and all can see is that same bed with the mysterious figure twitching as they lay.

'Excuse me,' I called out.

'Excuse me, are you okay? What happened? Why are you crying?' I said in my sequence of three, which was annoying. When I think about it; I am dreaming, so why does it still remain?

'I know you don't know me, but I am here to help, it will be okay. I promise…'

"Alexa, Alexa, breathe," I heard a voice call out, then everything around me began to change, the room was gone, it was black, and I was alone.

"Alexa, please," the voice echoed in the darkness that I was now trapped in. I started to concentrate on being able to see in the dark and suddenly, I saw Corbin's face in front of mine getting closer.

'Ewww… What the hell are you doing?' I said as I pushed off Corbin, feeling a little violated.

"Bless you, you're okay," Corbin blurted before hugging me tightly in his arms.

'Get off me,' I shouted at a heartbroken Corbin.

Corbin's eyes beamed at me. I could feel the pain I had caused him, and I could also sense I had offended him somehow, but why?

"I'm sorry," he said as he stood up.

'No, I'm sorry, Corb, I'm sorry if I offended you, it's just... that you caught me by surprise. I didn't know you felt that way, and you're a great guy, but you're like family to me. I see you more like a fatherly figure to be honest, not a boyfriend. Sorry again!' I responded as I rose to my feet.

Corbin's head sunk down into his hands, 'oh, my god!' I made him cry, I broke his heart. Well, this was awkward, I would have never imagined these turn of events. I continued to watch Corbin not sure what to do, his shoulders began shaking as he made a small humming sound, it was starting to freak me out if I'm honest. Without any warning, Corbin's humming changed into a loud laugh.

'Whoa, what is so funny? Are you okay?' I asked in a curious tone.

Corbin continued to laugh, then finally spoke as he tried to control his composure. "Alexa, I do not have feelings for you; well, not in that way, I do care for you... Well, like family too, and when you awoke, I was just about to perform CPR."

'So, you were going to perform a verse on me? I asked, confused.

"A verse? What? Jesus, no. I… CPR is Cardiopulmonary resuscitation; it is a lifesaving technique made useful in many emergencies such as a casualty found unconscious or not breathing. You weren't breathing, Alexa, I thought you to be dead," he explained.

'Oh, right!' I said, feeling a little embarrassed with the accusation I had just made.

'But Corbin,' I asked.

"Yes, Alexa"

'I thought the black book said I couldn't die?'

"Well, err, yes, it does," he replied, not sure of himself.

'So, why were you so worried?' I asked, sounding more like I was teasing him.

"I.... I," he stuttered, sounding overwhelmed and embarrassed. "Look, let's just agree to disagree. Anyways, are you alright?" he asked.

'Hmmm, if you say so, and yes, why wouldn't I be, why was I on the floor anyways?' I asked, then it hit me as my eyes left Corbin's and looked past him.

Dozens of bodies lying on the floor. I walked over to one, its face disfigured, mouth wide open with holes through its eyes. It looked as if it had seen a ghost or something.

'What have I done to you?' I whispered as a tear dropped from my eye.

"Alexa, are you alright?" Corbin asked.

'Yea,' I said, trying to clear the lump in my throat; the chunk of disappointment I felt within myself. I understand they were evil, but they didn't deserve to die that way.

"Good, we must move. I heard more on the next floor; the quicker we move, the quicker we can get this done and recharge," Corbin ordered.

'Sure,' I mumbled as I continued to stare at the bodies, the people who I murdered.

"Okay, and can we stick to the plan this time? I don't enjoy being nearly barbequed," he said before smiling at me. I gave him a faint smile back, I could tell he was trying to take my mind off it all, and I was grateful for it. Corbin walked further down the hallway to a staircase; I followed behind, my mind still on the Taken I just killed.

"Alexa!"

'Yes, Corbin.'

"Are you ready?" he asked.

'Not really! Just kidding,' I smirked to show I was okay.

"Very well; let's get this over with."

I've found myself often questioning time since this all happened. When you go through the things I have been through, you end up finding yourself challenging everything, then realize how much you took it for granted when you did have it. I realized how much I didn't appreciate it… how much I didn't appreciate the time, the idea of it. It's kind of frustrating when you have a task to eliminate something, and there is no change in the day/night to show how much time has passed.

Is this what hell is like? Going through an endless torment; no time, no age, and no change, just endless. If so, I pity the souls in suffering, especially the souls that were already in their own infinite pain before being sent to hell. I felt like I was in my own personal hell, murdering Taken after Taken, no idea on how much time had passed, no idea on how much more we had to go through; never-ending. I didn't understand why I felt this way towards them, I am the Savior after all, but I honestly don't believe I was created for this purpose. The book said I was supposed to save and protect many, what does that all mean if all we are doing is killing them? It didn't make sense.

Corbin and I were on the last floor of the building, luckily it was clear, and that was the end of my personal hell for that moment. We decided to stay at the top as it was the only floor without dead bodies and that metallic scent. It seemed like the best move, and if we were ambushed, we could escape from the roof and climb down the fire escape where Corbin moved the car.

It's funny we came all this way to search for a place to rest, and after all that fighting and trying to survive, we weren't even tired one bit.

'What are you doing?' I asked Corbin.

"I am trying to heat up a tin that we can share," he replied.

'Hmmm… Okay,' I mumbled.

"What is the problem?" he asked in a curious tone.

'Oh, nothing, I'm just bored.'

"Bored? We have just survived from going over 50 of the Taken; you should be shattered and grateful to be alive."

'Corb!'

"Yes, Alexa."

'Who told you how to find me? Or should I say what?' I asked, but Corbin remained silent as he watched the tin heat.

'You said you will tell me everything but as I remember, that is one thing you haven't shared,' I continued.

"That is one thing I do not wish to share," he replied, shutting down that topic, but I wasn't giving up that easy.

'Why? You have shared other things, even about the trials and tribulations you went through, like that guy, John, you met years back that nearly cost you your faith and chances as being a priest. You said you were so close to helping him, cover up a murder that was revealed to be a misunderstanding,' I blurted out.

"Yes, so…" replied Corbin.

'So, so why are you so secretive now? What is the big deal?' I snapped.

"Calm down, Alexa. I would like to keep my eyes; thank you very much," Corbin replied in a sarcastic tone. "Fine, if you must, I have been studying your life since I was a young child."

'You said since your adolescence and what do I have to do with your explanation?' I said, cutting him off.

"Oh, yes, I forgot you remember details; I must be precise from now on," he said while rolling his eyes. "Anyways, yes, if you let me finish. Oh, yes, the food is ready. Ok, ok, I will start; there's no need for the antagonizing eyes. I have been studying your life for some time now and even though I have, I never truly believed it until the day I was told you were found and even then I didn't honestly believe it till I saw what you were capable of. Now, my point is that, before I came for you before my father died, I believed, but I didn't actually believe. If that makes some sort of sense to you."

'So, what are you saying Corb?' I interrupted again.

"I am saying that there is a whole world out there of things that we do not know about and I had to learn the hard way when searching for you, Alexa. I came across things I never knew to be possible, I travelled all over the world for a way to find you. I learned about colts, witches, spells, demons. Then I heard of her…

'Her?'

"Yes, Ortora."

"She is a mixed breed of the Succubus and Laplace demon."

'Laplace?' I asked, confused.

"Yes, Laplace…. in the history of science, Laplace's demon was the first published articulation of causal or scientific determinism by Pierre-Simon Laplace in 1814." He explained.

'Ok,' I replied, not sure of his point.

"According to determinism, if someone (the Demon) knows the precise location and momentum of every atom in the universe, their past and future values for any given time are entailed; they can be calculated from the laws of classical mechanics." He continued.

'I am really trying, but I do not understand what you are telling me.'

"It wasn't something founded on a scientific path, the Laplace demon actually existed but was kept a secret."

'Err, ok.'

"Jesus!" Corbin muttered under his breathe. "Okay, let me try dumbing this down for you."

'Hey, no need to be rude.'

"LAPLACE DEMON IS A DEMON…

'Why are you shouting and talking so slow?' I said, cutting him off. 'You know what? Corbin screw you! That's right, I said it. I don't care who you are anymore. Because you know what your problem is, you have been on your own far too long to know how to interact with people and acknowledge their feelings, you are a mean, cranky, jerk when you haven't had any sleep as well. So, I think the best thing you should do is go to sleep. No, stop right there; don't even speak good night.' I snapped at him before moving to the corner of the room we were hiding in and faced my back to him.

"You're right…. I, Alexa, you. You are my friend, and I am sorry if I hurt your feelings. You are right, I am tired, and I've been on my own for a long time. Even before I returned, I was always on my own, just alone. It's been lonely; I forgot what it was like to have a friend, to be a friend until I met you."

I remained quiet as he spoke my eyes on the wall, my fists clenched as I tried to control my anger.

"I truly am sorry, Alexa, and I know I keep saying this but the things I've done over the years, makes it hard for me to be who I am, I always question who I am, if I am really good. Ortora; she made me question everything, she challenged me and often had me doubt myself. Hmmm, how does one fall for a succubus ey? So powerful, how she tricked me, how she made me believe… well, that is in the past now," he continued.

'You are forgiven, okay? Can you finish explaining about the Laplace?'

"Sure," he replied. "So, yes, the Laplace is a demon that knows the precise location and momentum of every atom in the universe, meaning it can sense anyone in the world. It was told that the demon existed centuries ago and was kept a prisoner for years and experimented on. Then one day it escaped but weak from whatever those scientists had done to it, soon after it met a succubus and, well, you know," he explained.

'Oh, I see! I mean I understand,' I replied, my eyes still facing the wall but feeling slightly heavy. 'Did you love her?'

"No," he replied. "Was I in lust with her? Yes, but I realized she was nothing but a demon and she just used me as her tool, had me doing her bidding, and yes, I did it for the information I required."

'How do you know someone else won't find her to look for me? What if that's how they found Jenna and me to begin with? What if she comes for you?' I blurted out as I drifted in and out of my sleep.

"She won't."

'How?' I whispered.

"Because she is dead…. I killed her. Alexa, Alexa... Good night."

I opened my eyes as I registered what he said then closed it again

It's dark, and it's cold.

Why am I here? What is that sound? Where is it coming from?

Oh, great, it's that same dream again, why do I keep having this same dream? Well, I'm taking control of this shit. I look towards the small bed with the mysterious figure twitching as they lay.

'Excuse me,' I called out, nothing but silence.

'Excuse me, are you okay? What happened? Why are you crying?'

Great! Even when I try to take control of my dream, I still talk in my sequence; I defiantly need to go counselling when this is all over.

I started to charge towards the bed, fueled with anger as I watch this stranger who continued to ignore me. Then suddenly, the feeling of anger disappeared, and I come to a halt right in front of the bed as a different emotion flooded my body, and now, I have the urge to protect this person.

'I know you don't know me, but I am here to help. It will be okay, I promise.'

'Look, from what I remember, your face is a bit... Well, you have no face, but it's okay, I won't judge you. Wait, what am I saying? How can you have no face but you're crying? This doesn't make any sense whatsoever.'

The mysterious figure remained silent as I rambled on beside them.

'So, you're really going to just sit there as I chat shit besides you?' I asked in an irritated tone.

'So, still nothing and I've taken control of my dream, and you still can't talk back, ey?'

The mysterious figure ignored my question but then suddenly I could hear a low humming sound coming from their direction. I sat there quiet and confused, I continued to listen to the humming; it was a song, and it seemed familiar.

'Wait, I know this,' I whispered as I stood to my feet. 'How do you know this, how?' I questioned.

The sound of the humming got louder and louder, as the figure began twitching.

'Jenna,' I whispered.

The figure stopped humming.

'JENNA!' I shouted, causing the stranger to spin around quickly.

“Who’s there?” said the stranger as they looked up and looked right through me, it was Jenna.

I sat up quickly gasping for air, inhale, exhale, breathe, Alexa; just relax. What was that? A dream, a vision, it felt so real. I looked around to see Corbin asleep, how long was I asleep for? He looked so peaceful, but I had to wake him at once, Jenna is alive!

‘Corb,’ I whispered as I walked over to where he was sleeping. ‘Corb,’ I called out again a little louder.

‘Really, Corb?’ I said in an irritated tone, how could he not hear me? What if I were being attacked?

I walked over to Corbin’s leg and lightly tapped it with my foot, but still nothing; it was like kicking a dead body, dead weight.

‘Corbin, ewww, what is that awful smell?’ I moaned out just as a whiff of the aroma hit my nose. Don’t worry, it wasn’t a metallic scent, so there wasn’t any Taken in sight but a nauseating odor; rotten and sickening. The embarrassing thing was that the smell was actually coming from me; I remembered after my realization that Corbin promised me a bath and fresh clothes, yet, here we are, and I stink. This angered me as I watched Corbin, I felt horrible, and I could no longer hold in my anger, I leaned over to Corbin and whispered ‘Wake up, Cathy.’

“HOW DID YOU DO THAT!” he shouted out as he jumped out of his sleep.

‘Do what?’ I asked sarcastically.

“You know what? You were in my head, in my dreams, you were taunting me with my middle name, and how I regret sharing it with you,” he said as he rose to his feet.

‘That’s not important right now, we need to go,’ I said as I started to gather my things.

"Why do you sense more coming?" he asked as I felt him watch me put on my shoes.

'Look, we don't have the time to discuss this, we need to hurry,' I ordered, Corbin nodded and started to put his jacket and shoes.

As soon as we were ready, we headed to the roof to exit down the fire escape stairs, the walk was silent, and we moved quickly and swiftly.

"I don't understand. I don't hear anything, where are they?" asked Corbin as we stepped in the car.

'Where are who?'

"The Taken, obviously."

'I never said they were coming.'

"Then why make us leave?" Corbin asked in an annoyed tone.

'Because I had a dream, Jenna's alive, we need to save her.'

"Wait, you made us leave because of a dream?" Corbin said, cutting me off.

'No, it's not just a dream but the same one I kept having, who's to say it's a dream and not a vision or even more than that. Corbin, there's something I haven't told you when we went back to the secret corner, and you left me in the tunnel, stupid plan, by the way. Anyways, as I was waiting, a few minutes later you came running towards me ordering me to run to the car, and I did, but when I got there and touched it, all the doors locked, then I lost my temper and told the car to open.'

"Alexa, why are you telling me this?" Corbin interrupted.

'Wait, I'm getting there,' I snapped. 'I made the car fly towards you and explode. Corbin, I watched you die, then suddenly I was in the tunnel again, and it never happened. But it did, I was there, it was real.'

"The Savior is Omniscient, all-knowing, hmmm…" he mumbled.

'So, my powers are amplifying; I can see the future but doesn't the prophecy say I'm omnipotent, meaning everywhere? What if I am, well, a part of me? What if that was a dream/vision at first and I projected there the last time? Corb, I focused really hard on her and called out her name, and she turned around.'

"Alexa, I don't doubt you at all, but that still doesn't explain why you made us take the roof instead of just leaving the old fashion way, right through the front door."

'My bad, Corb,' I said as I patted him on the shoulder.

"All is forgiven," he said while winking at me. "So, what is the plan, do you know where she resides?"

'That's the problem. No, I could only see a room when I was there,' I sobbed.

"Then I'm afraid there is nothing we can do yet, Alexa, I believe she is alive, but if we have no leads and we defiantly don't have the resources, we will have to wait till your powers hit its peak and you have full control," he explained.

'Never, I can't turn my back on her just like that, she needs me, and I need her, she's always believed in me, and now I must believe too,' I said as I was staring out the passenger window, then everything went completely black.

Caught in-between shock and shit scared, my heart was racing but no signs of breaths from my mouth. Darkness changed into a dim light, and now I'm in this hallway with the same metallic scent just like the building I was in. Where is this? Where is here? Baffled, I remained frozen, my heart still racing and no signs of breaths. I continued silent, muting my thoughts, opening my ears, heightening my senses. Through my left ear, I could hear light murmurs, I focused more, and they became apparent, a foreign language at first that began translating itself.

Two guards bickering, "I don't know why we can't just kill her already," said one of the guards.

'Shut it, it is Isaac's orders which came from Sir Michael, and we must obey,' replied the second guard.

Blocking them out, I stretched my focus; further, there was a door, and I could see it so clearly in my mind, the sound of a heartbeat, the sounds of shivering and clicking, and the sound of her humming the same song in my dream.

I transferred my focus onto my right ear, focusing on what was coming from the other direction; I could see a brown wooden door with a round, golden ball handle.

I could smell a high volume of metallic leaking through the door, I could see the one they call Isaac and then suddenly...

"AHHH... Where did you come from? Who are you?" shouted Isaac, who was sitting behind a big marble desk.

'You can see me?' I asked, baffled as I looked around to see if he was talking to someone else.

"What are you?" he moaned.

'I'm your worst fucking nightmare. Well, I will be if you don't give her back!' I ordered.

"What? You've come for the girl, oh, you must be the friend. I'm afraid I can't," he replied as he sunk in his seat like a frightened mouse.

'You don't want to make me angry,' I said as I clenched my fists.

"Please," he screeched before throwing an ashtray at me, which went flying through me and smashed to pieces against the wall.

Now let me tell you this; if you've watched as many movies as I do and have seen a lot with ghosts, like Casper the friendly ghost, a classic, everyone knows that one. Well, if you're like me and ever wondered what it may feel for that to happen to a ghost, I will enlighten you; it was the most uncomfortable experience in my life. It was like when you're eating fries or drinking a soda and the saying 'it went down the wrong hole.' Well, it was like that but amplified.

As Isaac watched the ashtray pass through me, a huge smirk came across his face,

"You're just a ghost and your giving orders," he said in a mocking tone.

'This is the last time I will ask you to give me the girl,' I said.

"Or what you going to do?" he teased.

'NOW!' I shouted, causing the window to smash with several pieces' fly through me into Isaacs's direction. Isaac jumped off his chair onto the ground; I followed as I walked around his desk and looked on to this pathetic man shaking on the floor.

"Alright, alright, what do you want?" he squealed.

'A location and the girl,' I replied.

"Are you crazy? I can't, we need her?"

'No, you don't, I'm the chosen one, not her.'

"He won't let you go if you came."

'Fine, a new deal, a trade; you can have me instead, but you have to release her and never go after her again, DEAL!'

"Yes, yes, just don't kill me please. I'll run it with the boss, but it should be fine. We are at an abandoned warehouse in Plymouth Avenue, Rochester.'

'Really!' I barked.

"Please, I'm not lying to you. I promise, you will know once you see it," he quivered.

'Excellent! That wasn't so hard, thank you for your cooperation, I will see you in a few hours. Don't mess this up,' I said as I walked away from the desk.

"I won't, I promise," he moaned.

A few minutes had passed, and I was still there trying to figure out how to leave, "hey you! Why are you still here? Shouldn't you be leaving?" said Isaac as I turned around and saw him peaking from his desk chair.

'Don't rush me, how dare you? I'll leave when I want to leave.' I began ranting on, all of sudden I was gasping for air, and I was back in the car.

I looked to the driver's seat; Corbin was nowhere to be seen.

'Corb…Corbin!!' I screamed.

I sat there quietly for a few minutes freaking out in my head debating with myself to stay and wait or leave and find him. More minutes passed, and just as I was about to get out of the car, the sound of footsteps was all I could hear.

'One, two, three,' I counted with my hand resting on the car door handle.

'Slam' went the sound of the lid of the boot of the car.

I listened to the sound of the steps as they walked closer and around to the driver's side door, I watched it open and studied Corbin as he sat down.

"Oh," he said. "You're awake."

'Awake… where were you?' I demanded.

"Well, you zoned out, so I went to retrieve some supplies," he replied.

'Zoned out… Really Corb? How could you just leave me like that? Anything could have happened,' I said in a frustrated tone.

"Well, I have been around you enough to know what that look means, and I wasn't keen on watching you for five minutes," he explained. "Besides, there was no taken in sight; we needed supplies, and I was only gone for five minutes, and look, here you are."

'Whatever! I still can't believe you, Corb!' I said while shaking my head.

"Well, I'm sorry, but yes, enough of that mushy stuff, what happened with you?"

'Right, how could I forget? We need to move now, I know where Jenna is,' I said as I looked out the window, and suddenly the car started without Corbin's key in the ignition.

"So, we're just going to ignore the fact that the car started on its own back there," Corbin said anxiously.

'Just keep your eyes on the road, and what's there to say? You've seen more than enough; I don't know why it still amazes you or that you still question it.'

"Hmm, true and I could say the same to you telling me to keep my eyes on the road. We've been travelling long enough to not worry about that kind of stuff," he replied.

'Touché'

Corbin looked at me from the corner of his eye, expressing a wink and a half smile while remaining his focus on the road ahead of us.

"So, you never said what happened to you, where did you go?" he asked.

'She's alive, Corb. All I remember at that moment talking to you, I was thinking about her and how she always believed in me, I realized I had to really believe. I owed it to myself and to her for having so much faith in me, then I wasn't with you anymore, I was somewhere else. The lights were dim, the walls were filthy, I can remember the smell of metallic and it was cold. I could hear her behind a door where they kept her, humming that same song. The guards outside bickering, and the one in charge hidden somewhere else.'

"Who Mi, Mi," he stuttered.

'No, not him, but his right-hand man which I didn't understand how, he was nothing but a coward. He told me where they are, I made a deal, and I offered myself for Jenna.'

"You did what?" Corbin blurted out interrupting me.

'Relax, Corb, it's all part of my plan. We arrive, I do the exchange, Jenna walks to you, I wave the signal, you shoot some down, I blow some away. We run to the car, and bam; that's how the Savior kicks ass with Corb, the ninja,' I said as I waved my hand in the air ready to give him a high five.

Corbin hesitated then lightly tapped my hand whilst still remaining his focus on the road.

"Are you sure about this? I have your err back. But I just want you to make sure you're ready."

'I'm ready as I'll ever be, Corb, well, to save Jenna. Could we at least save her and focus on saving the world after?'

"A hero doesn't save the world in a day," he said.

'Erm, I'll take that as a yes.'

'So how far are we away from this place?'

"Really?" said, Corbin, as he pressed his foot down on the breaks. "You haven't even said where we are going, we've just been driving," he continued in an irritated tone.

'Oh, right! We are headed to an abandoned warehouse in Plymouth Avenue Rochester.'

"An abandoned warehouse, is that it? How are we supposed to locate her with those instructions?" he questioned.

'Isaac said I would know when I see it, I know he wasn't lying, and I didn't push for more because I knew I would sense her, just like I was this whole time; it's strange,' I said as I looked into the night, inhaling the cool breeze, enjoying the touch of the air caressing my cheeks.

"If you insist. By the way, I've noticed you have been holding onto that book of yours since we got in the car, why have you not opened it?" he pressed.

'Err... Corbin, why have you not started the car? Why have you not answered my question? Do you want my YHDI to return?'

"NO,' he shouted. "I mean, no, please, no. No one wants that to return, believe me. So let's see, you said Plymouth Rochester… Well, lucky for you, I borrowed a car that is quite modern to your sort. Let's see, what do we have here? A CD compartment, radio, oh, yes, maps navigation. So if I insert here our destination of choice and have the GPS find us, okay, we are a few miles away from Parkville, and from Parkville, it is just about three and a half miles away," said Corbin.

'Great, why are all these places far away? I'm surprised that the GPS and all that still works considering the circumstances,' I pointed.

"Yes, surprising, but I believe it's to do with you and your powers, but enough of that, back to what I asked."

'Fine, I hold on to this book because it was the last of the books I had drawn in. I'm curious to know what lies on these pages, however, afraid as this was the one I drew the face of the demon that chased Jenna, the face of our friend. I'm just not ready to see,' I explained as I put the book into Corbin's bag and took out the black book.

Corbin nodded an acknowledgment of what I just shared and continued to drive; I opened the book and began flicking through the pages.

Each page more interesting than the last, fine details of God and his grand plan, the story of my life. Memoirs of what it seemed to be from ascendants of the Michaels. Details of the moment I was found, notes jotted down of my progress, sections about my weaknesses and my strengths. I continued to read page by page, speed picking up as I memorized each page after the next, thrilled with the knowledge I was gaining. Corbin remained silent, allowing me to study, as he continued to drive down this endless road.

A couple of hours had passed, so I had decided to take a break. I didn't say anything to Corbin; my mind was on Jenna, how all this time I was dreaming about her, sensing her pain. We are connected somehow, I could see it now, but why? How? It didn't make any sense.

I could feel Corbin looking at me with a sense of worry reeking off him, he cleared his throat then spoke: "Are you alright, you seem like you got a lot on your mind."

'You're right, I do,' I replied. 'And yes, I'll enlighten you. This whole Jenna thing, it's freaking me out. This whole time I was dreaming about her, Corbin, all this torment I've suffered in my mind was because of her, what could that all mean?' I continued as I started to flick through more of the book's pages. 'Jenna and I are connected. Why? I don't know, but saying it out loud is putting all the pieces together.'

"What do you mean?" Corbin pushed.

'Everything that has happened to us was not a coincidence, all those years ago when the head sister wanted her removed from the home, and I convinced her to act out of character with every visit. The head sister was so close to giving up until the last visitors came. I remember that day so clearly; there was something off about them, the way they spoke, the way they watched Jenna. How, you ask? I was hiding in a closet watching everything, and the man, he was so pale and creepily thin. He had his eyes on Jenna like she was a juicy piece of steak. Jenna did everything she could, but he was adamant about having her, and the way the agents took an interest to her, they even went after her instead of me,' I trailed off.

'The constant urge to protect her like she was this fragile, precious ornament.'

"What are you saying, Alexa?" asked an intrigued Corbin.

'I don't know, there's something... wait a minute,' I said, changing the topic. 'There's something off with this book.'

"What do you mean off?" asked Corbin.

'I….' I began talking then zoning out as my fingers trailed through the pages of the book, to the edges, across the cover, down the bottom, and to the middle.

"What is it?" Corbin asked, eager and intrigued.

'Some pages are missing. If you look closely, you can see it was torn; whoever did this tried very hard to hide it. You can see where the torn edges should have shown, they have been blended in the paper instead with a layer of gloss over it. Who would do this and why? 'I asked, confused.

"I have no idea, I had no idea, just great we have to save your friend, which we now learn is linked to you somehow and now pages from the book, or as you like to call it, the 'mysterious black book', has been missing, pages I never knew to exist. What if they are significant? What if you can die and the details are in those pages?' Corbin blurted out.

'Inhale, exhale, inhale, exhale. Calm down, Corb, you are freaking out as I've never seen before, I may not be able to die, but you sure can so keep calm and focus on the road, okay? We will figure this out,' I said trying to reassure him.

"My apologies, Alexa. I just wasn't prepared for this; I didn't prepare enough.'

'It's okay, Corb. Who could have known?'

"Alexa, may I question you?"

'Err sure.'

"What do you know of Jenna? You said you met in the home, but how long was she there? When did she become an orphan?" he asked, question after question.

'To be honest, Corb, I don't actually know that much stuff about Jenna's life before I met her. I remember I'd always ask when we were growing up, but she would always say she doesn't remember or want to talk about it, that it's a time of her life in the past and the past shall stay in the past. I would always say okay and drop it, then ask again, and over time, I respected her wishes and accepted her for just her.' I explained with a high feeling of uncertainty.

'When I think about it now, I don't know anything about her.'

"What else are you thinking?" he pressed.

'I think that between the connection I feel and the lack of knowledge of her past,' I hesitated as I rested my hand on the book where the pages should have laid. 'I think there's something about Jenna.'

"Alright, we are here. So the plan is, you will do the exchange, and the moment Jenna is by my side, you will give a signal. I'll take out a few guards, you go all glowy and blow them away, then we get the hell out of there. Correct?" said an eager Corbin as the car came to an abrupt stop.

'Err… correct,' I said feeling a little sick from the constant use of the glowy term.

Corbin loaded his gun while he stepped out of the car. I took a deep breath, 'well, here it goes,' I muttered just as I followed after him.

We didn't park too far just in case shit goes down and we need to get to the car quickly, so the walk wasn't too far, I could already see the building and the guards into the distance. I could sense her to and the urge to protect her returning so quickly, I could hear her heart beating so fast; she was afraid. Could you blame her? Look at everything she had been through, but she wasn't going to be scared any longer once she would see I am here to her rescue.

Whoever chose to keep her hostage here was a narcissistic fool; the setting was just creepy, I could see from afar on how scary the building looked, with its boarded-up windows. I was nervous, my palms were disgustingly sweaty, you'd think I was going on a first date or taking an exam.

As we got closer, we came to a small flight of stairs, three guards were waiting with Isaac hidden in between them.

"I see you've made it," he muttered. "I bet you wonder how I knew you would be arriving, don't you? Well, I have eyes everywhere," he snickered.

'I actually don't care, now where is she!' I demanded.

Just as I said that, I heard the sound of a door open with ten guards marching out, one by one and at the end, I saw Jenna, hands tied and frightened. Just as her eyes met mine, they lit, a sense of relief coming from her.

"So, we made a deal," muttered Isaac.

'Send her over!' I ordered.

"You come here first!" he ordered.

'No, not until I know she's safe.'

"For the love of god, can you both just walk over at the same time?" Corbin interrupted.

'Fine,' we both said in sync.

And with that, one of the guards cut Jenna's hands free and she began walking towards me. As we reached each other, she stopped right in front of me trying to hold back her tears. I looked at her patting her on the head, 'it will be okay, just go stand by Corbin.' Jenna nodded and walked towards him, and I continued to walk towards the guards listening to her as she reached Corbin's side.

As I got closer, I heard an unfamiliar voice whisper, "Once you have the chosen one, kill the others."

Shocked with what I heard, I spun around before reaching the guards, shouting to Corbin 'DO IT NOW, CORB!'

As soon as he heard my order, Corbin pulled out his gun and began shooting guard after guard right in the head. I turned back around and luckily went all glowy at the right time, throwing my flame at two more guards knocking them to the floor. Then, a sudden noise broke out like a roar and before we knew it, dozens of the Taken from different directions ambushed us, but that didn't stop us… Corbin pulled out his cross and pressed the button, transforming it into a sword; as I headed straight for Isaac throwing him through the wall which knocked him unconscious.

All of sudden, I've been knocked to the floor. 'ALEXA!' I could hear Jenna screaming in the background. What hit me? How did I not see it? I'm flat on the ground, legs shaking as I struggle to get to my feet, trying to figure out what just happened and as I look up, I see...

'Corbin,' I said in a baffled tone as I saw Corbin a few feet facing towards me, with a knife pointing in my direction.

"No, the name is Michael," the Corbin lookalike said.

'I, I don't understand,' I whispered as I rose slowly to my feet, with my hands in the air not sure to attack.

"It doesn't matter," he whispered just before he lunged to attack.

"No," a familiar voice said as they blocked his knife.

"Arr… Look who it is; my younger brother!" muttered, Michael.

'Corb,'

"Alexa, protect Jenna!" ordered Corbin.

Still confused in what was happening, I hesitated as I watched Corbin fight himself; I just didn't get it. He said his brother was older, but they looked exactly alike. So caught up with it all, I nearly forgot about Jenna. In reality, time was barely moving, my power was almost at its peak, and I was nearly in control, but it didn't matter because no matter how much control I had, nothing prepared me for what was next. The sounds of Jenna's screams sped up everything because when I looked around, I saw the Taken tearing her to pieces and just before I could react to that, the sound of a knife piercing through flesh was all I heard next. My eyes shifted back to Corbin, 'nooooooo!' I screamed as I watched Michael knock Corbin to the floor, Corbin's heart stopped instantly.

They were both dead and there with a smirk on his face was Michael, he was enjoying it, he wasn't going to get away with this. I could feel the bomb inside me ticking again, I was going to explode and not the kind I've been doing before, this was going to be something I don't think even I could come back from. Michael watched me, his eyebrows raised as he noticed the glow around me go more prominent. He seemed frightened at first, but that soon was forgotten when he ordered the Taken to kill me.

I looked behind me to a Jenna that was once there, I looked to a dead Corbin that never gave up on me. I watched as the Taken came charging towards me and let out a big roar as the flames left my body. It travelled so aggressively as it hit Taken after Taken, as it hit the building, as it hit Michael. I watched as they burned to their deaths, I watched as it burned Corbin and what was left of Jenna, I felt myself deteriorating into nothing.

"You still reading that book," asked Corbin. "Alexa!"

'It wasn't real,' I thought out loud as a tear rolled down my eye.

"What wasn't real," asked Corbin

'What?'

"You just said it wasn't real, what are you talking about?"

'Erm,' I hesitated. 'I just had a memory of something in the home, it's quite embarrassing, to be honest, I don't even know why I thought about it,' I lied. I couldn't tell him the truth, tell him that he died because of me; I had to fix this on my own.

I wiped the tear away from my eyes as I closed the book. 'So, are we there yet?' I said in a more cheerful tone as I placed the book back in Corbin's bag.

"Actually, it's up ahead, but I don't want to park too far but not too close if that makes sense," he explained.

'I understand, but could we stop here instead?' I insisted.

"Sure," he said as we pulled up to the side. "Alright, so we are here, the plan is."

'Yes, the plan is exchanging Jenna and I and blah, let's go,' I said cutting him off, not in the mood to replay what just happened.

"Very well," he said before stepping out of the car, not noticing my weird behavior. "Why are you taking the bag?" he asked.

'Just in case anything happens, you should carry it at all times,' I instructed.

"Okay, makes sense, and what about you?"

'Everything you, I mean, we need is in your bag,' I said, correcting myself not trying to give away my intentions.

"Okay. Well, let's get this over with," he mumbled before walking towards the scary building.

As we got close, everything was as it was in my vision; the wind, the cold, the three guards with Isaac hidden in-between them. I did as I did before and requested to see Jenna, ten guards exited with Jenna following behind. I knew Michael was around here somewhere, I kept my eyes on Jenna and Isaac so it wouldn't seem suspicious. I listened carefully; I could hear his breathing; he was hidden behind one of the guards. I could hear the Takens' bones clicking, hidden in between the trees and darkness; they were there, waiting so patiently, waiting to ambush us.

Before Isaac could debate with me, I instructed for Jenna and me to pass at the same time, Isaac nodded and ordered a guard to set her free. Jenna began walking towards me as I to her. As she came to me, she stopped. Before she could speak, I pulled her in close and gave her the biggest hug I've ever given in my life. I quickly whispered, 'I love you so much, you were the only family

I had, well, until I met Corb. Stay with him, Jen, he will keep you safe.'

I pulled away from her and patted her lightly on the head, Jenna nodded and continued to walk towards Corbin as I continued to walk towards the guards, I listened to her breathing and her heartbeat then she was by Corbin's side. I got as close as I could, moving quickly before Michael could reveal himself, and just before he could make the order, I dropped to my knees smashing my hands on the ground causing it to crack and separate Jenna and Corbin away from the guards, Isaac, Michael and I.

"Alexa," I could hear Corbin shout out. "This wasn't the plan."

'Kill them,' ordered Michael.

"No," I screamed, pounding my hands harder, as I watched them. They were covered in a white glow that was projecting following the cracks I made, creating a protective barrier around them just as the Taken were about to charge.

I looked at Jenna, her eyes were on me, those same blue eyes filled with horror, and then bam, I'm on the floor. How didn't I see that coming when I already didn't see it coming in the vision, and I still wasn't prepared for it. The glow around them started to fade, and I could see the Taken getting closer to them. Before I could react, I was being dragged off the floor by a guard, as he held on to my clothes. I grabbed his hand and twisted it behind his back before kicking him out of the way.

I looked back at Jenna, who was hiding behind Corbin as he fought for their lives.

"Corbin!" I shouted as I punched another guard out of my way.

"Alexa!"

'Hold Jenna's hand,' I instructed.

Corbin gave me a brief look before nodding as he took hold of Jenna's hand.

"Alexa, what are you doing?" cried Jenna as the Taken got closer.

'It will be okay, I promise,' I said as I looked in her eyes and waved goodbye to the both of them.

'It will be okay, I promise,' I repeated as I watched them fade away and vanish into nothing; I don't know if I killed them or sent them somewhere. I seemed to have sent Corbin somewhere before at the secret corner, so let's just hope it worked again.

My hand still in the air as I watched the Taken crash into each other. A small smile across my face as a tear rolled down my cheek, feeling some sort of satisfaction knowing I prevented their deaths, and then suddenly, I felt a small prick in my neck.

'Ouch,' I said as I looked beside me shocked to see Michael with a smirk on his face.

'What did you do?' I said struggling to keep myself standing, and once again, I could feel my consciousness slipping away…

'Owww, my head is spinning, where am I?'

'Jenna?'

'Corbin?'

'Someone!'

Why can't I move?

Just as I was about to scream my lungs out, I heard a door open, and a mysterious woman in a white coat walked in. A bright light followed awakening a white, padded room that I am in.

'Who are you? Where is she? Where is Jenna?

"Good afternoon, Alexandra, my name is Dr Sherman, and I will be assisting you with your recovery."

'Recovery? What recovery? Where is Jenna? Tell me!' I shouted, struggling to move, feeling restrained of some sort.

'Alexandra, I have no idea what you are talking about, who is Jenna?' she asked in a questionable tone.

'What? She's my friend, where is she? Tell me, where am I,' I argued.

"Alexandra, I'm afraid there has been some misunderstanding. I do not know of this Jenna, but you are currently in the physic ward for the mentally insane. You have been here for some time now, you had one of your episodes again and attacked the last doctor assigned to you, why you've had to be restrained." She explained.

'What, what do you mean mental ward? I am the Savior and I have to stop them, the...' I wondered off confused with what I was trying to say. For some reason, I couldn't remember and what she just shared didn't fully hit me until I looked down and realized I was sitting in a straightjacket...

TO BE CONTINUED...

Lightning Source UK Ltd.
Milton Keynes UK
UKHW011829170919
349958UK00001B/33/P

9 781916 193505